THE COUNTRY

BOOKS BY DAVID PLANTE

THE COUNTRY   *1981*

THE FAMILY   *1979*

FIGURES IN BRIGHT AIR   *1976*

THE DARKNESS OF THE BODY   *1975*

RELATIVES   *1975*

SLIDES   *1971*

THE GHOST OF HENRY JAMES   *1971*

THE
COUNTRY

DAVID PLANTE

ATHENEUM

NEW YORK

1981

A portion of this book originally appeared in *The New Yorker*
© 1980 by The New Yorker Magazine, Inc.

Manufactured by Fairfield Graphics, Fairfield, Pennsylvania
ISBN 0-689-11189-4
Library of Congress catalog card number 81-66002
First Printing August 1981
Second Printing October 1981
Third Printing November 1981

With love
to Stephen and Natasha Spender

PART ONE

I

ON THE TRAIN from New York I sat next to a young man with a blue shirt and long black hair. I looked past him and out of the window at factories and high chainlink fences, and then I looked at him again. He had pale, reddish-brown skin; he shook strands of hair from his face and smiled a little at me. His name was Jake Santuri, he said, and he was going to Kingston, Rhode Island. He asked me where I was going. "Providence," I said. He said, "You're not from around here. I can tell by the way you talk. Why are you going to Providence?" "I'm going to visit friends," I said, then, "relatives." The pupils and irises of his eyes were equally black. He said, "You ever been to Providence before?" "Yes," I said.

He told me that his father was Italian, his mother was American Indian. He said, "How's that for a combination?"

I smiled.

"Where are you from?" he asked.

I said, "London."

"In England?"

"Yes," I said. "I just got here."

His voice rose. "Hey, you just got here?"

"I come every two or three years on a visit."

"I'd like to go to London," he said. "I really would. Life must be different there. What kind of life do you lead there?"

"What kind of life do you lead here?" I asked.

Well, he didn't want to settle down, not yet, there was so much he wanted to do, but maybe when he did settle down he'd be a plumber or a welder or something like that, because he liked working with metal. He was almost eighteen; he had to start thinking about things like what he wanted to do. He'd got into some trouble, he'd spent two years in a reform school, but at eighteen you went into prison if you got into trouble. He had a friend Rocco, in prison, and he'd visited him, and that was hell.

He and Rocco and some friends, they used to do jobs for people who wanted to collect insurance on their cars, so these people would pay them, say, a hundred dollars to steal their cars and blow them up. He showed me how to make a time fuse with a cigarette and a book of matches. One time he took a car into the country to blow it up, and Rocco was following him in another car with the gasoline, but he lost Rocco on the way, so he drove the car into a field, and he ripped up the seats with a broken bottle and stuffed the car with dry grass and set fire to it, then ran like crazy through the woods, but stopped to turn back to look and saw the car filled with flames, and, just then, *baroom*, the whole thing exploded, and he kept running, running like crazy until he got out of the woods. He had to walk thirty miles into town.

I said, "Aren't you afraid of the cops?"

"Naw," he said. "They're so stupid. Rocco, he's my closest friend still, a tough guy, with thick hams, a real good runner. Once, he put boards with spikes in them all around a field near his house, and he lit a fire in the middle of the field just to attract the police, and they came in there with their cars, and you could hear the tires bursting. The cops got out of their cars and tried to catch him, and he got them running around after him, and when one of them tried to head him off, he ran right past him, and his mother was there, shouting, 'Run, Rocco, run. Don't let them catch you'."

I said, "But Rocco got caught."

Jake didn't say anything; he scratched his nose.

I said, "You like taking risks."

"Yeah," he said, "I like taking risks. I ride my motorcycle, boy, in a risky way. I've had some pretty close misses. I once drove off a cliff." He looked away from me and out of the window.

The train was passing a dump of crumpled, rusted cars piled on one another. He looked back at the dump as the train passed it.

He said to me, "I ran away from home once and lived in an old wrecked car in a dump for three weeks. I'd take girls there. They'd say, 'Is this where you live?' I don't know why I do, but I like dumps with old cars. I like railway yards, too. I like lumber yards, and I like brick and cinderblock yards."

I looked out of the window with him. We passed an old brick factory, derelict, its small windows broken, and among the weeds in the factory yard were rusted machine parts and by the railway tracks a heap of rusted metal, gears, shafts, flywheels. Jake said, "Hey, look at that." He turned to me. "Did you see that? I really like metal."

I smiled at him, then again looked past him, out of the window to a view of low grey-green land with dumped stoves and refrigerators, and beyond, the grey ocean where up-ended in the waves was the hulk of a battered tanker, and I thought, This strange country—

Jake was studying me. I didn't look at him until he said to me, "My mother would like you. She likes people who are different. You like fish? How about coming to eat with us? She'll make you a great fish dish."

I asked, "Do you speak any Indian language?"

He laughed. "Me? Naw."

"Tell me in what ways you're Indian."

"Well," he said, "all you have to be is an eighth Indian to

11

be officially an Indian, and I'm half—" Then he laughed so that lines curved in his cheeks, and he said, "I don't know."

Out of the window was a single square clapboard house and a row of bare trees in a field at the edge of the ocean; the white sun was high and the house and the trees and the field and ocean appeared plain grey.

I said to Jake, "I want to tell you I'm not a foreigner."

"What d'you mean?"

"I was born and grew up in Providence. I left when I was your age."

He glanced to either side of me, and after a moment he said, "That's all right, I'd still like you to meet my mother. Come to our house. She'll like you just the same."

"Thanks," I said.

"That's all right," he said.

When he got off at Kingston, I sat by the window and watched him descend from the train. He jumped over a low barrier into the station parking lot and lifted his old Army dufflebag to squeeze between two cars. His long hair swung.

As the train came into the station at Providence, I saw my brother Edmond on the platform, looking away. He had a bald spot on the top of his head. I got off and called, "Ed," and he turned around. Lines were in his face, and his belly bulged under his green work clothes. He opened his arms and came towards me. "Jeez," he said. "Jeez." He put his arms around me. He had an acrid smell of printer's ink. "My brother," he said, "my brother from a long way away." He released me and I lost my balance. He reached for my large suitcase standing beside me on the old wooden platform; his fingertips and nails were black from the ink. We went out to the parking lot. Providence in the spring heat smelled of raw dust and tar.

In the car I asked, using what I thought was an easy idiom, "How are the folks doing?" and then I thought, No, and I said, "I mean, how are Mère and Père?"

"They're better," he said. "You'll see they're better since three years ago."

We drove up out of the city, past the white dome of the State House rising from a hill, and, turning left, drove gradually higher, into Mount Pleasant. I looked out of the window with a sense of seeing things that were familiar but that I felt I had never seen before: the large blossoming maple trees along the sidewalks; the furniture store with a gleaming aluminium front and clapboard sides, cardboard cartons piled outside; a collapsed picket fence separating the driveways of two tenement houses; a brick public school-house fenced into its asphalted schoolyard, sheets of plywood nailed over its doors and windows; the trunk of a maple tree. It seemed to me that everything I saw stood out from itself in the sun's glare and I was seeing not the houses, cars, trees and people but their reflections.

I spoke, too, not to Edmond but to someone just to the side of him. I said, "Mère is all right, then?"

"Yes, she's recovered. Except her eyesight got bad with the last spell. She can't write, can't dial the telephone, can't see the hands of the clock, but she wants to see, and even says she thinks her eyesight is getting better."

"Will she be able to see me?"

"Oh, sure," he said. "But I'll tell you, it hasn't been long, her recovery. You know, last fall, around October, we thought she was going to die. She wandered around the house moaning. And then she took to hitting the walls. She was scared she was losing her mind. Père couldn't do anything. He'd just watch her. I'd sit with her and listen to her, just listen to her say—well, you know, the same old story, over and over, the same thing she's been saying, I guess, for

13

twenty years. I wouldn't say anything. I'd just sit there and listen to her until she'd get tired, and then, finally, she'd go to bed. But the next day it would be the same when I got back from work. Sometimes she'd get up at night, wander about the house moaning."

"You were very patient."

He said, "Sometimes I could hardly bear it, but I stuck with her. Then I have to do all the housework they can't do. I stuck with her for herself, but, too, for Père—"

I asked, "What about Père?"

"Well, there he is, almost eighty, and he stands as straight as he always did. But when I'd come into the house from the shop and find him watching Mère walking up and down the kitchen—"

He stopped at the curb under a great blossoming maple tree by a new chainlink fence. Beyond the fence and narrow weed-grown yard was the white bungalow. I sat in the car and looked at the two dark windows of the kitchen. In each, between the curtains, a pale face appeared, blurred by the aluminium screens.

I said, "There they are."

I sat for a moment longer, then got out. I opened the gate and rushed up the stoop to the back door, but it was locked. Edmond came behind me with his key. At the top of the entry steps, by the open kitchen door, side by side, were my mother and father—small, old. I grabbed my mother and held her, but I felt I might hurt her if I held her tightly. I drew back, and she appeared to search the air to find me, saying, "Oh." I turned to my father. He was looking out of the window. I put my hands on his shoulders, and he, looking not at my face but at the floor, patted my arms. I pulled him closer to me and kissed him high on his cheek. My mother, her head raised as if the tilt allowed more light into her eyes, said, "Why are you crying?"

14

"I'm not," I said.

Edmond was behind me with my suitcase. "Where do you want this?" he asked.

I was wiping tears away with my knuckles. "Put it by the stove," I said, and I opened it, all the while weeping. Edmond gave me a tissue from his pocket to wipe my eyes and blow my nose, which I had to do from time to time, as my mother, my father and Edmond stared at me. I took out the woollen lap rug for my mother, gave it to her; the long woollen bathrobe for my father, gave it to him; the woollen jersey for Edmond.

The sun was beaming through the pantry window into the kitchen; there was a block of yellow light on the wall above the table, set for supper with mismatched plates, glasses, a loaf of bread and a carton of milk. It was five-thirty.

My mother said, staring not at me but around me, "We hoped you'd get here for suppertime. We didn't fuss. We're having a sauce blanche."

Edmond served us the sauce blanche with a ladle from a pan into plates we held up to him; the flour paste and shreds of chicken spread over the plates. He sat across from my father. I sat across from my mother, and I watched her carefully; she leaned close to her dish and ate with a big spoon, and often when she raised the spoon to her mouth there was nothing in it. Her face was distorted with age—her nose a little crooked, her cheekbones prominent and one higher than the other, her eyes sunk into the sockets, her forehead large.

She put the spoon down, pushed her chair out from the table, and got up. My father, a fork raised halfway to his mouth, simply watched her. Edmond said loudly, "What do you want? I'll get it for you." My father said quietly, "Let her be." She, making a quick gesture with her hand, said, "I can do for myself." We didn't continue to eat until she came back

15

from the pantry with a pepper shaker, sat, and peppered her sauce blanche, but she didn't eat any more.

I noticed that my father's thin hand shook as he brought the fork to his mouth, and the food slid down his chin. His eyes, when he wasn't staring at my mother, filmed.

She said, "I was remembering the time Zouzou Blanchard came here—big fat Zouzou Blanchard, with hair on her chin—and after she left one of the boys smelled the seat of her chair and said, 'Ouf, mais il pue.'"

I tried to laugh. Her large forehead shone as she laughed. I said, "We never speak French any more."

Her face went dark. She said, "I promised your father's father, Pépère Francoeur, that I wouldn't let you lose the language. He told me, 'Ne les laissez pas perdre la langue,' and I tried, but we stopped talking French."

I said, "What are some old French expressions you remember?"

"Oh," she said, "let's think." I kept watching my father, who, paying close attention to her, didn't eat. He was frowning. She said, "I can remember my mother saying when she was angry, 'Sacrabe de vice. C'la parle au dioble.' That was 'diable' but she said 'dioble'. You see, I can be serious, too, when I want to be."

I said, "Père, your mother couldn't speak English, but could your father?"

My father looked surprised that I should be talking to him. He said, quietly, "A little." I waited. He put his fork on his plate. He blinked. He said, carefully, "Well, I can tell you this little story as an example of my father's proficiency in the language. Your mother and I were living over on Lester Street, in a tenement, and our landlord was a thirty-second-degree Mason, so he and his wife were, you might say, well off. My father came to pay his respects one day. Your mother and I were in the yard with the landlord's

16

wife. To be courteous, I thought I would go through the exercise of introducing her to my father, my father to her, and he said to her, shaking her hand, 'You're very welcome.'"

I laughed out. My mother raised her head to stare at me, as if wondering why I should be laughing at what my father said. She leaned close, perhaps to see better.

I said, "Père, did Mémère Francoeur know any language from her Indian mother?"

He said nothing for a moment. "Not that I know of," he said. "No."

I helped Edmond clear the table, and at the sink in the pantry he washed the dishes and I dried. Through the window above the sink I saw the spring trees along the street in the sunlight, the cars passing.

Edmond said, "How do you find the folks?"

"Well," I said.

He said, "She's all right now. It's Père I worry about."

I looked through the pantry doorway to where, at the kitchen table, my father was sitting. He had his glasses on, and he was examining the newspaper spread out before him. My mother passed before the table. She had put on a dressing gown and slippers. She walked slowly. My father watched her as she passed. Her back was humped. My father drew his hands to the edge of the table and looked down at them. My mother stopped before my father.

"What are you thinking, Jim?" she asked.

"Nothing," he said.

I came out of the pantry into the kitchen.

She said to me, "I've been married to him for fifty-six years and he's never told me what he's thinking." She said to no one, "We have so much to remember from our lives together, our lives with our sons."

He said, with a light laugh, "I don't remember anything."

She turned away. She walked as if her knees were locked

and she had to keep her balance with outstretched hands. She went into the bathroom and closed the door.

My father was against the light from the window, which appeared to beam about his dark head.

I said, "Père, let's take a walk."

He searched for where the voice came from. He said, "You must be tired."

"Yes, I am. I'm on a different time."

"And in a different place, too."

I smiled. "I couldn't sleep yet."

He said, "We could take a walk up to my sister Oenone."

"I'd like that. I'd like a walk through the parish."

He said, "The parish? The parish doesn't exist any more."

We walked slowly through the long warm sunlight past the clapboard houses, lawns and shrubs along what were called, I remembered, the piazzas of the houses. The houses appeared to be houses within houses, appeared to me familiar houses within unfamiliar ones. And the large, still, blossoming trees, too, seemed to me familiar trees within unfamiliar trees. And the sidewalks, cement or asphalt, were, I thought, raised above the sidewalks I recalled of bare earth with weeds growing along the curb and rusted tin cans in the weeds.

My Aunt Oenone wore about the crown of her head a neat braid of blue-white artificial hair held down by many pins; her own white, thin hair was wild.

She took from her mother's bedroom, where the large high bed was kept made, a little black valise, put it on the round oak table by the coal stove in the kitchen, and opened the latch to a heap of photographs. She put on a green visor, lit the ceiling light, made us sit with our glasses of root beer at the table with her, and passed the photographs to my father, who passed them on to me. He passed them without looking at them.

I held up to my aunt a brown photograph of a bald man with a long, unevenly white beard. I said, "That's Mémère Francoeur's father?"

She placed a palm over the eye with the cataract and leaned forward to look with one large eye. "Yes, le Grand Coq."

"There's no photograph of his wife?"

"Which one?"

"I didn't know he had more than one. The Indian—"

"No, she died, and he married again."

"Do you know anything about her?"

Matante Oenone said, "My mother told me le Grand Coq worked for a while in a lumber yard in Newmarket, Michigan, and one day he met a young Indian girl, and the Indian girl said, 'You've got a button missing from your shirt,' and le Grand Coq said, 'I know,' and she said, 'I'll sew it on for you,' and he took off his shirt. She sewed a button on and gave the shirt back to him, and he said, 'You'd make a good wife,' and she said, 'If you say so,' and they were married two weeks later."

"What language did they speak?" I asked.

She shrugged. "I don't know," she said. "From Canada he went down to Michigan, went down as far as California, to cut timber. But he was mostly in Canada."

"And what tribe was she from?"

"She was a Piednoir. Her name was Clyche."

My father, tapping the table with his fingers, said, "She was just a half-caste."

"She was a full-blooded Blackfoot Indian," Oenone said. "Her full name was Clyche Kirou. I have a copy of my mother's baptismal certificate that has her mother's name on it. I'll show you." She again went into her mother's room, and I saw her open the top drawer of a large black bureau with a lace runner on which were small painted statues of saints. She came out with a grey-yellow piece of thin paper, showed it to my father, who read it and passed it to me. It was written in pencil.

Extrait du registre des baptêmes de la paroisse de St Barthélemi pour l'année 1873.

Le vingt et un janvier, mil huit cent soixante et treize, nous, curé soussigné, avons baptisé Modiste, née ce jour du legitime mariage d'Adolphe Lajoie, cultivateur, et de Clyche de cette paroisse. Parrain—Alfred Mayer; Marraine—Marie Louise Flageole, qui n'ont su signer.

MG ARCHAMBAULT ptre

I said, "It just says her name was Clyche."

"Then maybe her mother's name was Kirou," Matante said. "Because my mother remembered her mother's mother—a big, dark woman with black braids. Every time my mother's mother had a baby, her mother came, laid the baby on a board, and bound it to the board with a long band of cloth, so Clyche could carry the baby on her back. And her mother, Clyche's mother, made moccasins. She beaded them, and to soften them she peed in them and left them under the wood stove for a night."

"How did they all get from Michigan to St Barthélemi, where the children were born?" I asked.

"I don't know."

"It's a bit jumbled."

"Well, that's what your Mémère told me. She said her mother smoked a corncob pipe and smeared her body in the winter with bear grease to keep warm. In the winter le Grand Coq traded with the Indians, who'd come into the house—they wouldn't knock but just opened the door and came in—and they'd go and sit on a long bench behind the wood stove and wait, and when le Grand Coq went to them they'd all mumble together. Your Mémère would go to bed, and in the morning there'd be a big bundle of pelts behind the stove."

I asked, "Do you know if Mémère spoke any of her mother's language?"

"No. I don't know. If she knew any, she never told us."

"Did she have Indian traits?"

"Traits?"

"Did she do anything that you thought was—well, Indian?"

"I remember her sitting cross-legged on the floor to braid her hair. Her hair was thick and black."

"I never saw our mother do that," my father said.

"I did. And she made cough medicine from sumac berries. You remember that, don't you?" she asked my father.

"Yes," he said.

"And she had a prayer—I don't know if it was Indian, but she had a prayer, and if someone were bleeding or were burned bad, she'd go into another room and recite the prayer, and the bleeding stopped, the burn went. You remember that, too," she said to her brother. "You remember the prayer."

"Yes," he said.

Matante Oenone said to me, "She taught it to him, the first-born son, and to no one else."

My father silently picked up the photographs one by one and looked at them closely.

"She couldn't speak English and she didn't know how to write," Oenone said, "so when she'd send us out to do some shopping she'd draw on a piece of paper what she wanted— she drew pictures of onions, pork chops, a bottle of ketchup, potatoes with the eyes, a chicken—and the grocer, Mr

Tetroux, could always make out what they were. She sent me out to the butcher to buy her a fesse de cochon, but the butcher couldn't speak French, and I wondered how I could ask for a fesse de cochon, and when I got there I said, 'Please, I want a pig's ass.'"

My father was holding up a stark black and white photograph of his mother sitting, her arms crossed, in a rocking chair, and he said quietly, "I remember a man delivered a big wooden washing machine to the house, but he couldn't carry it up the stairs to the top floor, and my mother said to him, 'Va t'en, va t'en,' grabbed the front legs of the machine, and carried it all the way up the stairs herself. She was a strong woman."

"She said her mother was so strong she could stop a runaway carriage just by grabbing the back wheel," Oenone said.

"Yes," my father said.

Oenone went on, "Her mother was—"

My father said, "Her mother died when she was only seven. She couldn't remember her that well. She died and Ma's father married Ma's godmother, Louise Flageole, who brought Ma up."

Matante Oenone began to put the photographs into the little case. She said, "I saw her—I saw our mother—last night. I woke up and I saw her standing, not in my room but behind the wall, in woods—"

My father got up. "Assez de c'la," he said, "assez de c'la."

My aunt stopped.

On the way back to the family house I said to my father, "I met a young man on the train from New York who said he was half Indian, he told me that if you're an eighth Indian you can be considered an Indian."

"Who by?" my father asked.

"I don't know. By the American government, I suppose. As an Indian you can make many claims—"

"Can you?" he asked, smiling.

"Well, if Clyche was a half-caste, your mother was a quarter, and you're an eighth."

He said nothing.

I didn't clearly see but sensed space all about me, light and dark, and the space, light and dark, kept shifting abruptly about, and for moments I didn't know where I was. It was as if I—in some other place, at some other time—had thought up everything about me, and everything might quickly change, and where and when I was would be very strange. I imagined I felt the sidewalk move a little under my feet.

"And," I said, "if Clyche was a full-blooded Indian, I'm an eighth; I'm a real Indian." I laughed.

Again my father said nothing. The sun was setting. The high light was shattered by the tops of the maple trees, and the trunks were in low shadow. We walked side by side. I wanted to touch my father.

He opened the door to the dim kitchen. My mother was in the rocking chair, and he went to her to lean over and kiss her, but she said, before he could kiss her, "You go away, I stay in this house." He stood back.

She rocked her body without rocking the chair. She said, "I'm where you want me to be, in the house. I've had to submit to this house like I've had to submit to your will. I've had to submit to your will like I'll have to submit to lying forever in my grave."

I stood by the door.

She said, "I always did what you wanted. You never cared what I wanted. You wouldn't let me have the operation, though the doctor said I should, said I'd die if I had another baby. I had seven sons. You kept me in this house with the children, you still keep me in it, you've had your will." She looked past my father. She said, "Who's standing by the door?"

I said, "I am."

She said, rocking her stiff upper body, "Your father has always had his will. He didn't want me to have the operation. I didn't have it. I did what he wanted. I always did what he wanted. He wanted us to sleep in the same bed, though he knew I couldn't have any children or I would die. And we were good Catholics, we didn't want to sin, we couldn't use anything to make sure I wouldn't have a baby. We slept in the same bed, but if he touched me I said, 'Do you want me to die?' He couldn't sleep, he couldn't work. I thought, 'I'm keeping him from sleeping; I'm keeping him from working.' I said, 'We'll sleep in separate beds.' He said, 'No.' It was hard. It was hard for him. It was hard for me. I thought, 'He can't continue like this.' I gave in. He had his will."

I said, "Momma, it's only because of my father's will that I'm here."

My father turned around to me, then he looked away, out of the window, where the dusk was deepening to dark.

My mother got up. She shuffled to the middle of the floor and stopped. She said to me, her voice small, "I submitted to your father's will to have you. I risked my life to have you."

I went to her. I put my arms around her. She didn't move.

When I let go of her, she said softly, "Promise me that I'll be buried upside down, because I'll try to claw my way out, and if I'm upside down I'll only dig myself in deeper. I'm too hateful to come back. I wasn't ever a good wife to your father, I was never the mother he expected me to be, I was never strong."

Slowly, she walked into the living room.

My father continued to look out of the window, where the

24

large maple tree was black. I went to him. I put a hand on his shoulder.

"I'm sorry," I said.

He shook his head.

"Maybe my coming back started up something in her," I said.

"I don't know," he said.

We heard her, in the living room, walking about.

"Is there anything I can do?" I asked.

"She'll be all right if she sleeps."

"Maybe I can do something. Maybe she'd like to talk to me. Shall I go in and try to calm her? I've done it in the past."

"No, no," he said. "She's my responsibility." He went into the living room.

In my old, small, hot bedroom, I lay naked on the bed. On the other side of the wall at my head was my parents' bedroom; our beds abutted on the same wall. The window was open, and the light from a window of the house next door shone across the hedge separating the yards and into my room, and from time to time a shadow crossed my wall. It seemed to me I was in the house projected by the light and the shadows, not in my own family house, and I didn't know the house I was in. I heard odd voices, low voices. Throughout the house of dim light and shadows doors opened and closed, and people passed from room to room. I saw, in a distant room, the bed of a couple, but empty, the sheets and blankets thrown to the floor. I heard doors opening and closing, and footsteps. I thought I heard a shout.

When in the night I woke, I lay wondering what I was doing in my parents' home. I wondered then why my home was now in a country that was not my country, where I was close in friendship and love to people unrelated to me—

people whose relationships to one another and to me I did not understand but whose relationships, in friendship and love, I tried day after day to understand.

I got up at dawn, and naked, with a numb morning erection, I left my room to go quickly to the bathroom. Rushing through the kitchen, I saw my father, and I stopped short, not knowing what to do; he, in his rocking chair, looked away.

Back in the bedroom I found in the closet an old bathrobe and put it on. I went to the bathroom, came out, and, drawing the robe about myself, I approached my father.

I asked, "Did she sleep?"

"No," he said.

"Where is she?"

"In her room. Saturday's often a bad day for her— Saturday and Sunday."

"Why don't we take her out of the house for the day? We can take her to the country. Wouldn't that help?"

"She won't go."

"She won't go to the lake?"

"She won't leave the house. She hasn't been out of the house for months. Edmond offers to take her out, and so does your brother Albert offer to take her out to his house in the country for as long as she'd like. She won't go. She hasn't been to church for six months, I think. She won't leave."

"Why?"

"I don't know. She keeps saying she wants to leave the house, wants to get out, but she won't."

I sat in the chair across from him. My bare feet sweated, and the palms of my hands.

I asked, "And how long has it been since you've really got away from the house?"

"As long as your mother."

26

I said, "Why don't you come out today with me? We'll visit Albert."

"Who'll stay with your mother?"

"Edmond will."

"He won't like that on his day off. He complains a lot that he has to take care of us."

"I'll ask him."

He pressed his lips together.

"Come on, Père," I said. "Just a couple of hours in the country."

He lowered his head. "She'll say I'm making her stay alone in the house."

"If she doesn't want to leave herself, does she expect you not to leave? She can't be that—" I didn't know what to say.

I saw him breathe in and out.

"Come on," I said.

His breath wheezed.

"Please," I said.

While he slowly put on a sweater and a jacket, I telephoned Jake Santuri; a woman with a high voice said he was out fishing. I said who I was. She said, "Oh, I'm Jake's mother." I said, "I'll have to go back soon." She said, "He'll be sorry. He liked you."

I put the telephone down and my mother asked, "Who were you talking to?"

"An Indian," I said. "An Indian woman."

My father sat up straight beside me as I drove Edmond's car; he looked through the windshield, never to the side, and I thought he was not seeing anything.

I said, "Dad, it'll do you both good to be separated for a while. She'll be all right."

He said, "I used to think she'd be all right. I'd go so far as to think she was well, and then, unexpectedly, she'd have a relapse. That happened over and over. I've given up believing she could recover with a little will power. I know that it is vanity on my part to believe she could, if she so wished, get herself out of her state when she is in a bad state. And yet she seems, when she is in that state, to be determined to stay in it, as if all her will power went into keeping herself in it, and she refuses to get out."

He stared ahead.

He said, "She never wanted children."

With a shift of my voice I asked, "Where did you learn English, Père?"

He said, "I was thought by the nuns at the école paroissiale."

He always said "thought" for "taught".

I said, "People say I have an accent. I think that's because I really don't know how to pronounce words, and I pronounce them as they're pronounced by people about me."

"I don't know," I said.

"And I have difficulty with prepositions," I said.

"What are they?"

"Small words like in, on, from, to."

"Yes," he said.

I drove in silence.

The rutted dirt country road, overgrown with grass because it was rarely used, took us along the edge of the lake and through the woods of pine trees and bare oaks and birches. Large brown ferns brushed the sides of the car.

My brother Albert was sitting on the screened porch of his house. He waved at us. A retired Marine major, he lived alone in the country.

We all sat on the porch. Albert gave my father a cup of tea.

He took it, placed it on an old painted wicker table, and stared at it.

Albert said, "I think Mère gets disturbed by our coming home. She gets disturbed by her sons' going and by their coming back."

My father said, "No, it's not her sons—"

After a while we took a slow walk down the drive. Small pine trees and birches grew in the lawn; there was more moss than grass. Last year's oak leaves, wet, were piled against the stone walls of the house. Down by the garage was a patch of wild irises and orange lilies in bloom, and across the drive from the garage were large laurel bushes that hid the old dock, rotted and listing. We walked up the drive around to the back of the house and into the woods.

I said, "I haven't been in these woods for years."

I went ahead of my father and brother to look. I passed the rotting frame of a canoe tangled in poison ivy. I passed a pile of old doors. I passed a rusted oil drum.

Sunlight beamed down through the trees and, as I walked, flashed across my eyes. It all at once seemed to me there were people in that light—naked, brown-red people hidden among the trees. They were familiar to me, familiar enough for me to sense that they were close. Yet they were strangers, too, because I could not see them and knew nothing about them. I had some remote claim to be among them. I imagined I could, by stepping through a shadow, find myself among them, but they would be like nothing I had imagined. They watched me, but they kept to themselves, and among themselves they formed a tribe in which their relationships were in no way comprehensible to me. I stood under a pine tree, sere blueberry bushes around me; I wasn't quite sure which way I should go. The woods were still, as the inhabitants were still. I pushed my way silently through the bushes.

29

I stopped, turned, and saw, in the light, my father, standing alone. He was very straight. He was looking away from me. His lips were moving. I saw, standing in the woods behind him, his mother, large and dark, and deeper in, a larger, darker woman, and then another and another, each larger and darker, mothers and daughters, daughters and mothers, going back and back, to a great dark mother, to whom my father could pray in a language I did not know.

II

A YEAR LATER, I returned. It was after dark, and my parents were asleep. I did not unpack. I went, too, to sleep.

I lay, after I woke, and looked about my old bedroom. Through the slats of the blind sunlight streaked in and created bright panes which, as I watched them, appeared slowly to rise and fall.

I slept a little longer and woke up to voices.

In the kitchen, I found my mother and my brother Albert at the table.

I kissed my mother.

She said to me, "You must be tired."

"I am."

Albert said, "Sit with us. I'll make you a cup of tea."

I sat with the cup of tea in the kitchen with all the blinds down, as the light hurt my mother's eyes.

My mother, in her padded blue housecoat, said to Albert, "Now see if I can remember." Her short white hair was uncombed.

"Try," Albert said.

"Let's see," she said. She put a finger to her wrinkled chin. "Oh Lord God—" She shook her head. "Now what is it?"

"Try to remember," Albert said.

She stared at him, her pale eyes bulging to see him, as if to see him would be to understand him. "What?" she asked.

Albert said calmly, "Think."

"Oh my God," she said.

"Lord," he said.

"What?" she asked.

"The prayer begins, Lord—"

"I can't remember." She leaned towards him to see him better and she concentrated. "Lord, make me an instrument of peace."

"That's fine," he said.

"I can't remember it," she said. "It makes me so angry. Oh my God, thy peace is an instrument."

"Not quite," Albert said.

She said suddenly and quickly, "Lord, make me an instrument of thy peace."

He laughed. "You've done it, Mom."

She smiled.

Albert said to me, "That's the longest sentence she can say."

"Momma," I called.

She put her hand out to me, but couldn't see me; I took her hand and held it.

She said, "It's nice you're home."

I asked, "Where's Père?"

"In the living room," Albert said.

"What?" my mother asked.

"He was asking where Père is," Albert said in a loud voice to her.

"Where is he?" she asked.

I went into the living room which, too, was dim. My father was sitting straight upright in a big wing chair, hands folded on his lap, his eyes wide open; he stared at me as I came towards him, his mouth a little open, but he said nothing. His plaid woollen shirt was unbuttoned, showing his undershirt.

I said, "Père."

32

My father's breath was wheezing. The lid of one of his eyes was turned in, and rimmed with yellow matter.

"I thought I'd come to find out how you are."

In a very short breath, just long enough for him to expel the words, my father said, "I'm all right."

"Père," I said louder.

My father tapped his chest. "I can't talk."

"You should try."

He kept his hand on his chest. He looked down at his shirt and after a moment he tried to button the buttons, but he did not seem able to bend his fingers.

Looking up at me, he said, "Will you button my shirt?"

I stepped away from him as to step away from his body.

"Will you?" he asked.

I crossed my arms at my waist. "You can't do it?"

"No."

I could not touch my father's body. "It doesn't matter, does it, that it's left unbuttoned?"

My father lowered his hands to his lap.

I held myself more closely about my waist and sat on a chair next to my father and watched him.

My father looked out into the dim room, his face stark, and while he looked out he picked at his thumbnail with the nails of his other hand. As if he had been unaware, then was suddenly aware of someone by him, he turned his head to me.

After a long while, I asked, "What is it?"

He said, "The nail of my thumb is broken."

"You can't cut it?"

"I can't, no."

"Let me see," I said, and took his hand. The nails were yellow and long and some of them were cracked. I said, "I'll cut them for you."

My father didn't answer.

In the medicine cabinet over the bathroom washbasin I

33

found a clipper and nail scissors. I took a towel, too, which I placed over my father's knees. He held out one hand, and I grasped it at the wrist, and I clipped the nails. One hand finished, I placed it on my father's knee, and he raised the other to me.

I asked, "What about your toenails?"

My father, as if stunned, said nothing.

"I'll cut your toenails."

"I'll have to wash my feet."

"No, don't worry about that," I said, and I bent further over to untie my father's shoes as he lifted each foot in turn. I pulled off his shoes and drew down his socks. The narrow feet were very white; the toes were twisted. I spread the towel under them. I took the sole of his right foot in my palm and turned round to hold his foot under my arm so I could cut the nails with the scissors; it was like cutting horn.

I blinked to rid my eyes of tears.

When I finished I put my father's socks back on, and his shoes, which I tied.

I asked, "Is there anything else you want me to do for you?"

"No, sir," my father said.

I stood for a while before him. I said, "Père."

"Yes."

I frowned. "You know who I am, don't you?"

"Yes, you're my son Daniel."

"You mustn't say sir to me. I should say sir to you. You're my father."

He said nothing. With the dustpan and brush, I swept around my father, who watched me, his eyes wide.

When I sat by him again, my father asked, "Are you writing a book?"

I smiled.

My father looked past me and I turned round. My mother

34

was coming into the living room. Many pins were pinned to the front of her housecoat. Her hair stuck out about her head. She stopped just inside the room and held her arm over her eyes to try to see.

I called, "We're here, Momma."

She said, "It's so bright in here."

I got up and drew the blinds halfway down the windows.

She shuffled into the middle of the room. "Where's your father?" she asked.

"He's right here, in his chair."

"I couldn't see him in the bright light."

She shuffled towards him and leaned over him. He looked up at her.

"Don't you want to rest now?" she said to him.

"Yes."

I helped him up from the chair by putting my hand under his arm; he lost his balance, however, and had to sit back before he rose, alone, to his feet. He went into his bedroom, off the living room, and closed the door.

My mother came very close to me. "I'm so tired," she said.

"I know. You should go into your room and rest with Dad."

Her face slowly twisted. "I want to die, I'm so tired."

"No, Momma."

"Yes," she said, "I do."

I said sternly, "No, Momma, you don't want to die."

She suddenly smiled. "No. I don't. I don't want to die."

"You go rest," I said.

She went slowly to the bedroom door, opened it slowly and, inside, closed it slowly.

I went through the kitchen into the pantry where Albert was peeling potatoes over a newspaper spread on the counter.

Albert said, "I realized I had to do more for Mère and Père than I'd been doing. I've got to be here while Ed is away at the printing shop. Then Ed hadn't been feeding them well. I've got to come down to the city every day to cook."

I took another knife from a drawer and began to peel a muddy potato; the mud streaked the white as I peeled.

Albert asked, "How was Père's conversation?"

"He had to pause a lot to get his breath."

"He was coherent?"

"Yes, he was."

Albert stood away from the counter, a potato in one hand, a knife in the other. "You know," he said, "his mind is further gone than Mère's."

"What?"

"You'll see. Mère plays games. You have to be patient not to get angry with her, because you know she's playing games. Père isn't playing games when he doesn't know if it's morning or evening."

"I see."

"Ed found him one night, in his undershirt and pants, wandering about the house, talking to himself. He didn't know where he was. He thought he was in his mother's house."

"Yes."

Albert said, "He's not too well physically, either. I have to help him with his bath."

"I see," I said.

"I think he'll die soon."

I sat reading in the living room. When I heard the door to my parents' room open, I went to it quickly; my father came out, and he looked about, dazed.

I said, "Can I do anything for you, Père?"

"No," he said, "no."

He sat in his chair in the living room while I read.

He said, startling me, "You shouldn't give up writing books."

I didn't know what he meant.

He tilted his head against the chair back and closed his eyes when my mother came out of the bedroom; pinning the safety pins on her housecoat she wandered about the living room to adjust the blinds and curtains to keep out the light.

In the grey cellar, my brother Edmond showed me the model trains. The intercurving tracks, the little houses and shops and post office and fire station and church of the town about the tracks, the golf course and the public pool, were laid out on plywood under a low bare bulb. One train, then two, raced about the town, and as one went under a stone tunnel another rose over a railway bridge, with a pond under it. Edmond, who was fifty-one, was at the controls.

He said, "This is how I spend my Saturdays. When I'm not working or doing for Mom and Dad, I'm down here with my trains."

"You don't see Tommy any more?"

"No. You know, we used to do a lot together, Tommy and me, we'd go up to the shopping mall and play the pinball machines, have an ice-cream soda, and I'd buy him a model car, then we'd go to his house and watch television with his mother, or he'd come home here and we'd watch television. But then when he became sixteen he bought a real car. Now he goes off on his own. I don't know where he goes. He was a good friend for a while, and I know that if I didn't use to have his company I would have gone crazy, with work and what I have to do for Mère and Père that Albert doesn't do, but now he doesn't come around any more."

"He was a nice boy."

"He was a good kid."

I went past old furniture, tables and chairs and a big sideboard and a gas stove, stacked together and grey with dust, to the back of the cellar.

Light from a window high in the cement wall fell in a block on my father's wide work bench, and in the light at the edge of the bench were vises; in one vise a piece of wood was clamped, the long plane by it, and around the plane and the vise, and on the cement floor, were thin wood shavings. The bench was littered with tools. A smell of grease rose from them.

Leaning against the end of the bench were long smooth planks of wood with smaller pieces of wood resting against them.

I called to my brother Edmond, "When did Dad last work on his table?"

"About three months ago."

"Do you think he's up to finishing it?"

"Gee, I don't know, Dan," Edmond said. "He doesn't seem much interested."

He stopped his trains in their tracks and came over to the bench; he picked up a short piece of wood from the parts of the table and examined it as if he were not sure what it was.

Edmond said, "Philip got him started on it. He said to me, Philip did, that he asked Père to make it to give him something to do, he shouldn't sit and do nothing all day. But it got to be that whenever Philip came down of a Sunday from Massachusetts and asked Père if he'd done any work, Père'd say he didn't have the time, so Philip stopped asking him, and he left it to Père to say if he'd done any work or not. He can't do much. He doesn't have the breath. Though on some days he has more breath than others."

Edmond put the piece of wood back.

"It doesn't seem to need a lot more work," I said.

Edmond picked up a flat small piece and turned it over;

this was more incomprehensible to him, and he placed it back.

"I don't know," he said.

He went back to his trains.

I said, "Hasn't anyone offered to help Dad on it?"

Edmond didn't hear.

Beyond the work bench, along a wall, were ladders, disassembled scaffolding, old tires, and a low black tool chest. The tool chest was splattered with different colours of paint. It had belonged to my father's father. When I opened it, a smell of metal and oil and dust rose up. In oil-dark sliding compartments, it contained wooden planes, spirit levels, instruments for simulating wood grain, lumps of blue chalk and dirty chalking lines and plumb lines and weights; at the bottom, oily, were saws and the heavy tool for threading pipes and bits of cast iron. I picked them up and put them back.

I wandered about the cellar, then went upstairs.

My father was sitting in his rocking chair by a kitchen window. Outside the open window the large maple tree on the dirt sidewalk was rounded with green-yellow blossom. Blossoms, in sudden small currents of air, drifted against the window screen; the air made the curtains move and brought into the kitchen a smell as of fresh water.

I sat at the kitchen table to continue a letter I was writing. Sometimes I raised my eyes from the paper to look beyond my father's head out of the window at the maple tree; then I focused on my father, who didn't rock, but sat still. I wrote a paragraph without looking up, and when I did I saw my father staring at me as he had been staring into the air. His face was stark, his jaw set so the bite thrust it forward. I did not know why he was looking at me.

I said, raising my voice because my father had difficulty hearing, "I'm writing to a friend in London."

My father blinked. The eye with the turned-in lid teared.

I said, louder, "I'm writing to London."

My father looked away as if he had seen something in the air of the kitchen which had got his attention.

It came to me that my father was a ghost against the bright window.

I called, "Dad."

He didn't move.

"Père," I called.

He turned his head towards me.

"Are you all right?"

"All right?" he asked.

"I wondered."

"Yes," he said, "I'm all right."

I put the pen down on the paper. I said, "You're breathing more easily today."

Frowning, as if he did not want to be disturbed, my father said, "Yes, I am."

"I think it's because I opened the window for the air."

"That may be, but your mother will say there's too much light."

"She can stay in her room for a while."

"She's in our room?"

"Yes."

"Will you go see how she is?"

My parents' bedroom door was ajar. I pushed it open to see, in bed in the stuffy room, my mother asleep. Her false teeth were out and her mouth was caved in. Her eyelids fluttered. I watched her for a while, then closed the door and went back to my father.

"She's asleep," I said.

"What?" my father asked.

"Elle dort."

My father nodded.

I sat again at my letter. But I looked up often at my father against the window.

"What're you thinking about, Père?"

My father shrugged his shoulders.

"You can't say?"

"I was thinking," he said, "of working on the table."

"Do you miss working?"

"I haven't worked in so long."

"Yes, and do you miss it?"

"I do."

"You got a lot from it."

"I liked my work at the file shop. I was fortunate," my father said; "I liked my work."

To keep him talking, I asked, "You didn't always work in the file shop, did you?"

"No."

"When did you start working?"

My father did not understand why I was asking him, but he said, "I started after I graduated from the French school." He wiped his tearing eye with the tip of his forefinger.

"How old were you?"

That his son was asking him made him open his eyes; the white brows over them were long and wild. "Don't you want to write your letter?" he asked.

"I'll write it later."

"I was thirteen. The legal age was fourteen."

I pushed the pen and paper away from me. "What was the job?" I asked.

The moment I asked the question, I wanted to get back to writing the letter; I didn't want to listen, because I was not interested in my father's world of work. I thought: But I am interested, I am.

"I applied at the Riverside textile mill," my father said, "and they allowed me to work though I was under age. At

41

fourteen I got my working papers. I was in the spinning room—" His voice suddenly stopped, as he did not have enough breath. He breathed in. "I can't talk properly."

I drew the paper towards myself and picked up the pen.

I wrote: I want to write about being with my father, but I don't want to be with him.

Once more I dropped my pen. I said, "Talk slowly."

My father breathed in deeply and said, "I worked in the textile mill till I was eighteen, and then I was fired."

"What did you do?"

"Well, I had a friend from the French school, George Girard, and he had a job at the Nicholson file shop. Workers there were making fifteen piastres a week, a good pay. They worked only from eight-thirty to five. Everyone wanted to work in the file shop. Georgie took me down with him, and he introduced me to his foreman, a Mr Rawley, a Jicky. He spoke with an English accent. Mr Rawley told me there was nothing for the moment, but he said he'd tell Georgie if anything came up. The next afternoon, a Friday, Georgie came to my mother's house and said Mr Rawley had told him to tell me to report for work on Monday."

"So you started work at the file shop."

"Yes."

I realized that my father's world of work had always been unknown to me because I hadn't wanted to know it.

My father put his arms on the arms of the rocking chair and raised his body.

"I was trained as a tool cutter in the XF section. Mr Rawley got me to learn the uses of all the machines. He liked me. He'd support me if ever there was any little difficulty. He'd come up to me at my bench, there among the other trainees and the experienced men, and he'd say, 'Jim, it was a lucky day you came.' When I became a full-fledged tool cutter he talked to me about being a foreman, you might say to prepare me for some eventuality, but, of course, the other men in the section didn't like that."

"No," I said. I didn't want to hear more.

My father put his hand on his chest.

"During the First World War I was made an Industrial Soldier. I wore a little pin. Because he knew I had some experience with chairing meetings, Mr Rawley asked me if I'd chair a shop meeting, during the fifteen-minute lunch break, to agree among us to collect fifty dollars for each one of the men who was being drafted so he could have a last good time before he was sent off. And we agreed that whenever someone was killed, a collection would be made and flowers sent to the mother or widow."

I asked, "Where did you learn about chairing meetings?"

My father frowned.

I repeated, louder.

He said, "In the party."

"What made you join the party?"

"Mr Rawley got me interested. As he was English, he couldn't vote. When an election came up, he told me I should vote Republican. I said I hadn't ever voted. I voted, for the first time, Republican. Mr Rawley got me interested in politics. I went with him to ward committee meetings. I got more and more interested. I spoke at rallies, in French and English. I went once to Woonsocket to give a speech in French. I got a big cheer."

"What was your platform?"

"I always spoke," he said, "against high taxation, inflation, unemployment, and for the right to work."

"And you believed the Republican Party stood for that?"

"I believed it and I still believe it."

"Did you bring your politics into your work?"

A tear was dripping from my father's right cheek. "Why did you ask that?"

43

"I wondered."

"I did in the shop what I believed was right as a worker in the shop. When the CIO and AF of L, in the Twenties, were passing around pamphlets to get workers to organize themselves, Mr Rawley, a superintendent then, came up to my bench and asked if I would help organize a meeting of workers to vote for an independent union, not affiliated with the CIO or the AF of L. I did, right on the shop floor. Mr Rawley was there, but he stood at the door and just watched. The workers voted for their own independent union. Mr Rawley, from the doorway, made a sign of approval to me. The meeting lasted exactly fifteen minutes, not a minute over our lunch break."

"And what happened?"

My father breathed in and his chest expanded; he tapped his expanded chest with his index finger.

"I," he said, "I became chairman of the Grievance Committee. The men would come up to me and say they had a grievance. I'd ask, 'What is it?' They wanted to smoke while they worked. I got management to agree that the workers could smoke while they worked."

"And then what happened?"

"For years the union remained unaffiliated. Then Mr Rawley retired, went back to England. He came up to me to say goodbye. The other men didn't like this. Somebody else took Mr Rawley's place. We didn't see eye to eye. He was Irish. I went to him with a grievance. He said to me, 'Do you represent the union?' I said, 'I'm chairman of the Grievance Committee.' He said, 'I'll only listen to a real union. Go get yourselves a real union.' He talked to the men himself. A meeting was held. I didn't attend. They voted for affiliation, and as soon as they were affiliated they went on strike."

"For what?"

"I don't remember. They went on strike. I didn't approve. I held out."

"You went on working?"

"I broke the strike. I did what I believed was right. I believed that the work was important. I went on working."

My father paused for a long while, breathing. He stared. I said, "So you were fired."

His face was tense. He said, "I wasn't fired."

"No?"

He said, "No. No one was going to fire me."

My father, sitting up straight, looked at me.

"I see," I said.

Slowly, the lids of my father's eyes began to close, and as they did his focus lengthened or shortened and he was no longer looking at me; his eyes closed, he held his head up, his long thin lips pressed together, as if concentrating on a pain.

I said, "Père."

He opened his eyes as slowly as he had closed them. I was not sure if he brought me into focus or not.

"What is it?" I asked.

He shook his head a little. He said, "I was fired."

"Yes, I know," I said.

"It was the Irishman who fired me. He was an infiltrator. Once the union was formed in the shop, he headed it. I was fired."

"I know," I said.

My parents did not go to church. Albert told them that, as they were old, they did not have to. If I had said to my brother Albert that I did not believe and did not want to go to church, he would not have reproached me; but I knew that for Albert not believing was not a reason for not fulfilling one's duty, which was beyond what one believed. Sunday

45

morning, I went with my brother to the brick parish church among clapboard tenements on a hill.

The congregation was small, and there were wide spaces between people so some had to walk the length of a pew to reach the nearest parishioner when in the Mass they shook hands. I recognized relatives and men and women who had been at the parish school with me. The pastor, a broad, grey man I did not know, spoke in English; it was only in announcing the names of the dead for whom memorial Masses were to be said that his pronunciation was French. That, and the French names painted on scrolls at the bottom of the stained glass windows given by the donors, was what remained French in the church.

At the end of the Mass, Albert and I left quickly; we did not wait to speak to relatives. The car was parked by the abandoned parish school. Albert drove past the hairdresser, the drug store, the laundromat, the bar, the drygoods store, the tenements and bungalows, the fire station and the post office. Along the sidewalks were maple trees and wooden posts strung with sagging wires. I saw, down side streets, at the ends of streets and behind broken chainlink fences, train tracks, and beyond the tracks a long low brick factory with a water tank on it. The factory had painted on it, in faded black letters on white, THE NICHOLSON FILE CO. The windows were boarded.

Albert parked under the maple tree before the small white bungalow.

My parents were sleeping, and Edmond, in the living room, was reading the comics. He held the comics close to his face.

Albert said he would cook Sunday dinner.

"I'll help," I said.

"No. You're still on the wrong time. Go and rest."

In my old bedroom, I lay on a bed. The room, since it had

46

been mine and my younger brother Julien's, was called the middle room, and used partly to store useless furniture from other rooms: a large console radio and phonograph, a black-and-white television, a desk, floor lamps. The bed I had shared with Julien was gone; there were two beds, one small, the other bigger, pushed against two walls, and pictures taken from other rooms hung on the walls. There were, all in a row, framed studio photographs of the seven sons, my six brothers and myself; there were framed studio portraits, too, of the families of the three married sons, and, separately, of nephews and nieces in graduation caps and gowns.

Lying on my stomach, I tried to write my letter.

Once in this house, in the parish, my thinking took on the shape of the house, and there was no outside.

I woke when Edmond came in and sat on the edge of the other bed.

"My brother," he said.

"What is it, Ed?"

"It's nice to have you home for a while."

"Thanks."

"I was wondering if later today, when you've rested, you'd like to go up to the shopping mall. I know you wouldn't be very interested in the pinball machines, but we could have an ice-cream soda."

"I'd like that, Ed."

"Would you?"

"Yes, I would."

"You don't remember, but when you were little, you and Julien, I used to take you out. Sometimes I used to take you down to the train station, of a Sunday afternoon, to see the trains come in. Do you remember?"

"Yes, I do remember."

"Albert told me to tell you it's time to eat."

Albert had boiled meat with carrots and potatoes.

47

My mother, looking around the table, at which I imagined she saw my father and his sons as at a great distance, said, "Who's missing?"

Albert said sternly, "No one's missing."

"Someone's missing," she said.

I said, "Maybe my being here has confused you."

"No," she said. "Someone's missing. Where's Julien?"

"Julien's in Boston," Albert said. "You know very well he's in Boston. Now I want you to stop this."

"What?" she said.

Edmond said loudly, "Julien's in Boston. He's been living in Boston for years."

"He's in the cellar," she said. "Tell him to come up and eat."

I said, "He's in Boston, Momma."

My father, as if unaware, blew with pursed lips on a large spoonful of stew and ate it.

My mother, a little angry, said, "Why don't you get him?" and, weakly, she called, "Julien, Julien."

Albert said, "Let it go. I think she's putting this on."

"Jeez," Edmond said.

"What?" she asked, squinting.

"Nothing," Edmond said.

She ate.

The kitchen door from the back entry opened; my brother Philip came in, and behind him his wife Jenny and a daughter. Philip wore a narrow-brimmed hat. I got up to shake my brother's hand, and as I did I leaned close to him; we let go of each other's hands and we embraced, clutching each other's shoulders. Then, a little embarrassed, we drew back from one another.

"You're looking very well," Philip said.

"And you."

I kissed my sister-in-law and my niece.

48

Edmond made room for them about the table.

"You see," my mother said, "someone was missing."

"How are you doing?" Philip asked her.

"I don't want to say," she said.

Jenny smiled wanly at her, her head tilted.

"And you, Père, how are you?"

My father lowered his spoon. "I'm all right," he said. His voice was weak. He stared a little at Philip, as if not quite sure who he was. The rim of the lower turned-in eyelid was red. He smiled. He said, "But I'm afraid that I haven't finished your table."

"That isn't why I came down, Père," Philip said.

My father raised a hand. "It's only taken me five years to get it so far, give me another five years to complete it."

I said, "While I'm home, I'll help you with it, Dad."

My father laughed, a small, heaving laugh. "What? And take away the next five years from me? I'm living to finish that table, and the longer I put off finishing it, the longer I'll live."

"I'll make sure you never finish it."

"You take your time," Philip said.

"I'll finish it," my father said. "I'll finish it."

My mother said, "To tell the truth, I'm not feeling all that well."

"I'm sorry to hear it, Momma," Philip said calmly. He was thin and handsome; he had a broken nose. He was an engineer and lived with his family in a large house in Massachusetts.

"How about my bathing you?" Jenny asked her mother-in-law. "How about me helping you to bathe?"

"I've brought you a box of bath powder, Mémère," Antonia, the niece, said.

"That's nice. I don't think I really want a bath."

"Come on," Jenny said. She got up, and Antonia, too, taking from her shoulder bag the round box of powder.

"Go ahead," Albert said.

"I never had daughters," my mother said. "I always had sons, son after son. They couldn't do for me what a daughter could have."

"You don't expect a son to bathe you, do you?" Jenny said.

Jenny and Antonia, one on either side, helped her into the bathroom, from which, now and then, one of them came out for towels. Whenever the bathroom door opened there was the sound of running water.

The sons sat about the table with their father.

My father said, "I hope you're not upset when your mother gets funny."

"What's that?" Philip asked.

Albert said, "She was acting up a little before you came in. We ignored it."

"I know her," my father said, "I know what she can get up to. She was pretending just now. I know when she pretends."

"We know, Père," Albert said.

Our father said, "I was never good for your mother. She was never happy with me. I know what caused her spells. I know."

"What did?" I asked.

His breath wheezed. "Her spells came after every baby was born."

Albert said, "Père, if you're the cause of Mère's breakdowns, so am I, so are we all. We've tried our best to make her happy. You have and I have and we all have. We can't do it."

"No."

We watched as Jenny and Antonia, one at each elbow, helped my mother from the bathroom, through the kitchen, and into her bedroom. She was wearing a housecoat, a pink one, and her head was wrapped in a towel. She was talking lightly, quickly.

50

Edmond cleared the table; he brought the dishes into the pantry and put them by the sink. The dishes all had different patterns: one had flowers round the rim, another was plaid, another was plain green, another was white with a blue edge. He cleared, too, the milk glasses, the carton of milk, the bread and margarine.

My father said, "Well, they can say what they want to me, they can use whatever foul language they want, but I know what I'm doing."

We were silent and still.

Albert said, "Yes, Père."

My father's voice rose. He tapped his chest and frowned. "No one's going to pull the wool over my eyes. No one. I know what I'm doing."

Philip reached out and touched his father's hand and his father looked through him.

"You do what you want," Philip said.

My father's eyes widened, and he focused. He said, "Philip."

"Yes."

My father said nothing; then, after a while, he smiled a little. "I thought I was in the file shop."

"That's all right."

Edmond was standing at the end of the table opposite my father. He said, "He goes off like that. We don't know where he is. Sometimes I think he won't come back."

"What were you going to do at the shop?" Philip asked in an intelligent, calm voice.

"I suppose," my father said, "what I always tried to do. Set the place right."

"You gave it a good try."

My father passed his fingertips over his forehead; his shirt cuff fell far down on his thin arm.

He sat up straight. He said, "I did what I could."

"You did."

He said, "I was telling Daniel about the file shop."

"We had a long talk," I said.

"I was telling him about Mr Rawley, the Jicky. I suppose, now, he's dead. He went back to England. I suppose he died there."

"You never can tell," I said. "I should try looking him up when I get back."

"I'll never forget when he came to me and said the old man wanted to see me. I shut off my machine and took my overalls off and hung them up and went along into the old man's office. The old man said, 'Jim, you're your own man. I want to ask you, as your own man, what you think we should do to save the shop from strike after strike.'" My father raised himself a little straighter, and, for a moment, kept his jaw out. "I said, 'There's only one thing to do.' The old man asked me, 'What's that, Jim?' I said, 'Fire everyone. Fire them all, and get out.' And they did what I said. And that was the end of the shop. They did what I said, and they closed the shop."

"Yes," Philip said.

Albert said, quietly, "You told them, Père."

Our father looked down.

"That's what you've got to do," Edmond said, "that's the only thing to do with those unions. I'd never belong to the Printers' Union. Never. They'd tell me what to do, they'd tell my boss what to do. The boss would sell up and go somewhere else, and what would I do? I'd be left out. What do the unions think we are?"

"That's enough," Albert said to him.

"I'll go see how Momma's getting on," Philip said. He got up and went out.

"Those unions," Edmond said, "they think they can tell you what to do." His saliva spurted.

"Assez," Albert said.

Edmond went silent.

My father's head was lowered; the hair was long at the back of his neck.

"Are you all right, Père?" Albert asked.

He didn't move.

"I'm going to go down the cellar," Edmond said.

"Are you all right, Père?" Albert asked again.

Edmond opened the door to the cellar and closed it after him.

"Père," I said.

"He'll be all right," Albert said. "I've seen him like this. Let him be and he'll be all right."

"I'll sit with him."

"If you like."

Albert picked up a cup of tea from the table and went into the living room.

Near my father, I said, "Père."

He raised his head; his eyes were brimming. He said to me, "I've been a bad man."

I stood and leaned over him. He was not able to shave properly, and under his chin and on his neck were patches of long white hairs. His eyes over-brimmed. The one with the infolded lid was half closed. With a little moan, as if to expel enough breath to speak, he said, "I have."

I held my father; I pressed the side of his face against my face.

My father said, with many long breathless pauses, "I have done no good, none to your mother, none to you boys."

"Père," I said.

"I have done no good in the world."

"Père, Père, you have worked so hard."

"For no good."

I rocked him back and forth in my arms as he wept against

the side of my face. He then kissed me, on my neck, just below my ear. I held him more tightly.

When I drew back I saw my father's contorted face. He reached into his trouser pocket for his handkerchief, wiped his eyes and cheeks.

Jenny came into the kitchen. She said quietly to me, "Do you want me to help?"

Weeping, I couldn't answer.

Jenny went away and returned with a wet face cloth. She said to me, "Here, wipe your father's face." I took the cloth and wiped my father's face; my father closed his eyes so I could wipe over them, then he stared out, and his eyes again brimmed with tears.

Behind Jenny, my mother shuffled up to us, asking, "What's the matter?" Her hands out, she pushed me aside. My father said nothing, and I did not know if she was seeing him. "Jim," she called. "Jim."

"Yes," he said.

She leaned close, her hand out to touch his head; she leaned closer and kissed his forehead, then she turned away.

Jenny said to her father-in-law, "Come join us in the living room."

"In a minute, when I get my composure."

"Come now," she said, and put an arm under one of his to help him up.

He walked, stumbling a little, with one hand over his eyes.

Albert met them at the living room door. He said, "You'll be all right, Père. You'll be all right."

In the kitchen, my mother said to me, "What's the matter?"

I took her arm to bring her back into the living room. I said, "You've got to help Père."

"Help him?"

"Yes."

"How?" she said. "How? You don't know how different it is. He doesn't hear me when I talk, and he does things I don't like, I say nothing, he puts his dirty handkerchief on the table while we're eating, I say, 'Jim, put your handkerchief away,' he doesn't hear me, I take it, I can't do anything else, but it doesn't matter, I'll be dead soon, I want to die." Her face twisted up.

"You've got to help him by being well even if you're not well," I said; "by being cheerful even if you're not cheerful."

"Do I?" She looked up at me.

"Yes."

She smiled a large false smile that showed the gums of her false teeth. She nodded. "I know," she said, "I know. It's what everyone tells me. Then I'll smile. If it helps, I'll smile. You see." She smiled at me again.

"I'm glad," I said.

"But nothing can be done for him," she said.

As we went into the living room, Philip and his daughter Antonia came towards us. Antonia took her grandmother's arm and said, "Mémère, come and chat with us." Philip said to me, "We'll go into the kitchen. I want to talk to you."

"What's going on?" Edmond asked, coming up from the cellar. His eyes were wide open, so all the black irises showed.

"Nothing dramatic," Philip said. "Nothing to get dramatic about."

"I heard crying. Was Père crying?"

Edmond followed Philip and me into the pantry.

His hands held one with the palm up and the other as in a blessing, Philip said, "The last time I came down on a visit, Dad told me the same, that he's a bad man. I thought, But this is my father saying he's bad. I tried to reassure him, but it was difficult."

55

Edmond was licking his lips and half forming the words he wanted to say. He shifted his weight from one foot to the other.

"I don't know," Philip said, "if this is some final vision Dad has of himself. We know it isn't true. We can't allow him to have it. If you could, while you're home—"

Edmond said, his voice raised, "I know what's wrong with Père. Albert's not strict enough with him. He's not strict enough with Mère, either. Now, when I used to be the only one to take care of them, I treated them proper. I treated them like they are. Père's a child. Mère's a child. I made them eat their food."

I said to Philip, "What do you think I can do?"

"If you could—"

Edmond said, "You've got to treat them like children. I know. If Albert wants to treat them different, he can, but he'll be the one to take the consequences."

Philip left us by the pantry sink.

Edmond said, "I used to tell Père, like you'd tell a baby, 'Stop this crying now, stop it,' and he'd stop."

I said, "Let's go into the living room with the others."

Julien, my younger brother, came in from Boston. He was large and dark, and when he stepped forward to shake my hand and smile, he seemed, too, to step back.

Julien's face was broad, his eyes black, and the deepest layer of his skin, red-brown and slightly oily, appeared to show through.

I said, "How are you, Julien?"

"Fine, fine." He stretched out his long arms, then put his hands at the back of his head, and his chest expanded. "I'm fine."

I knew that he would not say if he were not fine.

"I came down thinking I'd take Momma and Dad out for a ride," Julien said. "I thought they'd like to get out of the house."

"It is a beautiful day," Jenny said, as if a little embarrassed to bring in the outside.

"It is," Philip said.

The sunlight came into the dim living room in fine bright lines which formed the outlines, within the dark house, of a frail house of light.

"It's so glaring out," the mother said.

"You could put your sunglasses on," I said.

"The glare comes in around them."

"Come on, Momma, you haven't been out for so long, and you should."

Albert asked his father, "Would you like to go for a ride?"

"Me?" his father asked.

"We could drive up to the lake," Albert said. "I'd make you tea at my house."

"What does your mother say?"

Angry, the side of Albert's mouth rose on his clenched teeth, and he said, "Never mind what she wants." He pointed at his father. "What do you want?"

His father didn't answer.

"We could all go up to the shopping mall," Edmond said. "It would be my treat."

"It'll be cold out, too," my mother said.

We were sitting around on large, bulky armchairs. My mother was in one which tilted back, and she had pillows under her head and a lap rug tucked about her legs. No one looked at her, but at our father.

She said weakly, "I feel it'll be cold out."

"What would you like, Père?" Albert said. "Let us know."

"I don't think your mother would like to," my father said.

Again, Albert bared his teeth at the side of his mouth as if

57

he were about to issue an order, and he said, "I told you to tell us what you want to do."

My father folded his hands.

Albert said to Philip, "I've got to be a little severe with him. I've got to make him use his will. He doesn't."

"You should tell him what to do," Edmond said, "that's what you should do."

"Well, Père," Albert said, "tell us."

Julien raised his large hands. "I thought it'd be nice for us to go out for a while," he said; "I didn't want to force anyone."

"I'm not trying to force Père," Albert said. "I'm simply trying to get him to use his own will."

Julien put his hands on his knees and leaned towards his father, and they stared at one another.

"Tell us," Albert said.

"I'll go if your mother goes," my father said softly.

"All right, then," Albert said, "we'll go."

"What?" my mother asked, as though suddenly frightened.

"We're going up to the country," Albert half shouted.

"Who?"

"You, Père, all of us."

"Me?"

"Yes, you."

"But I had a bath, I'll catch cold, and I'm not even dressed—"

"I'll help you dress," Antonia said.

"We'll dress you warmly," Jenny said.

"I don't know."

"You're going, Mère," Albert said, "you're going, and there are no ifs and buts about it."

"If I have to," she said, "if I have to."

"You have to."

She smiled. She said, "If I had a will of my own—"

Antonia said, "We'll help you put on some make-up, too."

We went in three cars. The streets of the neighbourhood were deserted on Sunday afternoon, and the small blossoms of the great maple trees fell through the streaming sunlight on to the streets, forming the outlines of the trees in yellow-green patches. Julien drove our father in the first car. I was with my mother in the last car, driven by Albert. Some front yards had been seeded for lawns, and around them were stretched string fences with strips of white cloth to keep away the sparrows. A man was clipping a hedge. In the back seat, my mother talked without stopping, in sentence fragments; I half listened, and looked out of the window at the houses and the yards. Beyond hedges and fences were flowering forsythia and lilac bushes. My mother said, "What I always say, well, open arms, you hold them, your sons, with open arms, who was it? I can't remember, said that?, that's what I say, open arms, they come, they go, and I, well, I left my parents, didn't I?, hold them with open arms, you know what that means, don't you?" "Yes, I do," I said. In a driveway, in the sunlight, a dog was lying flat; it raised its head as the cars passed, then lowered it. "It means," my mother said, "now let me see if I can explain it—"

We drove up by the golf course and out of Providence into the areas of old clapboard houses on the edges of woods. Perhaps I was tired; I could not focus on what I tried to force myself to focus on. I saw, in the spring light, shapes, yellow-green. The car stopped and the little jolt made me re-focus, so I saw at a railway crossing a long low unpainted house with a porch and rusted tin advertisements for beer and cigarettes nailed to the side; as soon as the car started, I saw again a shape. I tried to concentrate on the white house with black shutters surrounded by a white picket fence, on a red barn, on the gasoline station with one old pump, and I wondered if these were objects from which the shapes, the blurred oblongs, derived, or if the objects were momentarily derived from the shapes. And as I looked more, the used-car lot with its overhead strings of pennants, the old brick school, the new house with a picture window, folded back into the woods.

Albert turned off the country road on to a dirt road which took us deep into the woods. While my mother talked, I continued to look out of the window. The woods were close, and among the bare oak trees were the pines. The light was thick among them.

The roof and stone side of the house appeared at the end of the rutted road. Albert went past it, and up, around the drive, from where the clear blue lake opened out under the clear blue sky, to the back of the house, where he parked by the other cars under a clothesline hung between two high pine trees.

I helped my mother out of the car into the sunlight. We all stood still in the sunlight. My mother put on her sunglasses.

"Let's walk a little," I said.

Supporting her, we walked towards the lake. About the lake the oak trees were in fine red blossom, and were reflected in the blue.

I said, "Now breathe in the fresh air."

She breathed in. Her small body was unsteady, and as she breathed she had to hold more tightly to me.

She stopped breathing and, startled, suddenly asked, "Where's your father?"

"Dad is—"

"Where is he?"

I looked round. My father was standing alone, facing the lake. His jacket hung off his shoulders, and his white hair, combed flat, was thin.

"There he is," I said.

"Where?"

I helped her to turn to look. She bit her lower lip. Then she said, "What if he died?"

I, too, looked at my father.

My mother called, "Jim."

He didn't hear.

"Jim."

He stepped backwards, and just when he appeared to stumble he righted himself; he turned to his wife.

She drew her arm from mine and held her hand out to him. He came towards her, slowly; she kept her hand out, and when he was near her she put her hand under his arm. They walked down the gravel path to the lake.

Albert called from the door of the house, "Where're Mère and Père?"

"They're taking a little walk," I said.

"We're having tea on the porch," Albert said. "Where's Julien?"

"I don't know. He probably took a walk in the woods."

Later, on the screened-in porch, where my mother sat in a shadow, I watched my father and Julien, outside in the sunlight.

Albert refilled the empty cups.

"What are they talking about?" Philip asked.

"Who?" my mother asked.

"Dad and Jule."

"I don't know."

Edmond was drinking a glass of milk. "I remember," he said, "when I used to take Daniel and Julien out, Daniel'd talk and talk, like Mère, and Julien, just like Père, wouldn't say a thing, and you couldn't tell what he was thinking."

Jenny said, "He looks a lot like your father."

"Not like me," my mother said. "Daniel looks like me."

"Yes," I said.

"I love them both the same, of course, I love all my sons, you know, just the same, I love them too much to want to, that is, keep them with me, I hold them all with open arms." She held out her arms.

I said, laughing a little, "Perhaps Dad is instructing Jule in the Indian prayers his mother taught him."

"What prayers?" Antonia asked.

"Nothing," Philip said. "It's just a family story."

"Yes," I said.

In the grey mid-week morning, I found my father at the kitchen table. His hands were over his face. Before him was a plate and a knife and a large white tea cup.

My father didn't move when I sat at the table with him.

I was frightened.

With a little spasm, I got up to see if my brother Albert had arrived since Edmond left for the printing shop. Albert hadn't come yet. The door to my parents' bedroom was closed, and I stood for a while before it, but I could not open it. I went back to the kitchen. My father's elbows were on the table, his hands over his face.

Again, I sat at an angle to him.

I went rigid when my father lowered his hands and grasped the edge of the table.

"Would you like more tea?" I asked him. My voice was high, and it startled me.

"No," my father said.

"Is there anything you'd like?"

"No."

My father was sitting with his straight back away from the back of the chair. His nose was large, his black eyes close, and his cheekbones were high and prominent. The lid of the one bad eye was swollen and half shut.

"Let's do something together today, Dad," I said. "Let's go down to the cellar and work a little on the table."

"I don't want to, tsi gars."

"Oh, don't say that," I said. "Don't say that. We'll work together on the table."

"I won't be able to."

"You tell me what to do and I'll do it."

My father didn't move.

"Please," I said.

"I can't."

"Please, please."

My father's eyes were focused, and his voice was, too. "I can't," he said.

I was trembling. "Please," I said. "You can't not do anything. You've got to—" I didn't know what to say. "You've worked so hard all your life."

My father appeared to wince a little.

"You can't just stop. You can't."

My father ran his hands over his lowered head, then raised it. "Very well," he said.

I helped him down the steep curving stairs into the cellar. Through the wet windows, the grey light moved. I followed my father to the back, near the furnace, where his work bench was.

"Sit here, Dad."

I brought forward an old chair that had been used for cleaning brushes, so it was painted in pale overlapping layers of blue, white, yellow.

"I'll be all right," my father said, but he sat.

I did not know what I was doing. I tried to appear to my father that I knew, but I didn't. It seemed to me my uncertain gestures were spasmodic. I was very frightened.

"Right," I said. "We'll have a look at what there is. Can you see, Dad?"

"I can, well enough."

"I'll put the light on."

"If you want."

I pulled a long dirty string to a rafter above the work bench and lit a bare bulb; its yellow light appeared to move in the grey light.

"We'll see what we have," I said. "We'll see."

"Let's first get the tools we need," my father said.

"You tell me what the tools are and I'll collect them."

"We'll need the mallet."

"Where is that?"

"In the chest."

I found it in the bottom of the chest. "And?"

"The mortise chisel."

"What's that?"

"It's on the bench, there. And the brace is there with a metal box of bits."

I drew them to a corner of the table.

"And give me the rip saw," my father said.

"What's a rip saw?"

"Give me the saw there," my father said. He held it up to the light and sighted up its edge, then put it across his knees. "It'll have to be filed and set."

"I'll do it."

"Do you know how?"

"I don't know what filing and setting a saw means."

Very slowly, my father rose from the chair. He carried the saw to the end of the work bench and inserted it, upside down, in a long narrow vise.

"We need a file," he said, and he tried to open a large drawer in the work bench, but couldn't. "Open it for me, will you, tsi gars?" he said.

I pulled at the metal handles of the drawer; it didn't give, and I pulled with my weight until it opened, filled with black

64

tools. My father took out a long flat file and laid it along the top of the saw; he bent to examine the line of the teeth under the file, and I bent with him; the teeth were uneven. "It'll have to be topped," he said. With short thrusts of his arms, he filed some of the points blunt. He put the flat file in a compartment of the drawer and chose a long thin file with three faces; he chose, too, a wooden handle and shoved one end of the file into it. His jaw set, he began to file the blunted teeth into points.

"Shall I do that?" I asked.

My father couldn't answer. The file made a high grating noise. I saw that, though his mouth was closed, my father's breathing was quick and shallow.

"I'll do it," I said.

My father gave me the file and stood by and watched.

I stopped. "Am I doing it properly?" I asked.

My father nodded.

I crouched to examine the teeth. "I think that'll do." I looked up at my father. "Don't you want to see?"

"It'll do."

"Perhaps you don't want to continue," I said.

"We'll continue as long as you want to. Now find the saw-setting pliers."

"What're they?"

One by one, my father lifted tools from the deep drawer and placed them on the bench until he found the saw-setting pliers; then he put all the other tools back.

"What does that do?" I asked.

"You don't know?"

"No."

"It bends the teeth of the saw, alternate ones in opposite directions, to set the saw."

"I see."

I didn't see.

My father adjusted the pliers and started to work; he had difficulty getting the tool in place, and his face tightened as with slight pain when he squeezed it.

"Let me do that," I said.

As I worked, my father said, "Not so fast, tsi gars," and I slowed down.

I did not want, however, to continue the work.

My father said, "The cutting edges of the teeth have to be sharpened."

"With what?"

"The saw file."

"The triangular file?"

"Yes."

I picked it up.

My father tried to catch his breath. "File alternate teeth," he said, "and use the same pressure and the same number of cuts at each tooth, and file straight across the blade."

Filing, I sensed fine vibrations up my arms.

My father sat.

"Now the saw's got to be reversed in the vise and the same done to the unsharpened teeth."

"Do you want to go upstairs?" I asked.

"No. I'll be all right."

I kept on filing; whenever I paused I heard my father breathing.

Albert came towards us through the moving grey and yellow light.

He said, "Hey, this is something to see."

My father stood.

"I think I've finished this, Père," I said. "What next?"

The filed teeth were metal bright on the rusty saw.

"We can do a little work now," my father said.

"Really something to see," Albert said.

I took the pieces of wood which were against the side of the bench and laid them across trestles. Some were wide, some narrow. The shorter pieces I lay on the longer. Dust rose about them.

"Do you have a plan?" I asked my father.

"In my head."

"And all the pieces for the table are cut?"

"I've got now to make the joints."

"Is that hard?"

"It's hard, yes. Do you want to stop?"

I did. I did not want to build a table.

"Of course he doesn't," Albert said. "You want to get the table finished, don't you, lad?"

"Of course," I said.

"Very well," my father said quietly.

"When I came in," Albert said, "I found Mère wandering about the house, wondering where you were."

My father said, "Is she all right?"

"Yes. She was just wondering where you had gone to."

"I should go up to see if she's all right."

"She is."

His face tense, my father said, "If she's not, I'll do what I can for her."

"I tell you she is."

"What do you want to do first?" I asked my father.

He picked up a short narrow piece of wood. "We can start with this."

"Give it to me, Père," Albert said.

He laid the length of wood on the bench, and with a square drew a line across the side and edge with a wide flat pencil; he cut along the lines with a short knife. Then he inserted a piece of wood in the wood vise.

I thought, maybe Albert will take over the work.

"Now where's the marking-out gauge?" Albert asked.

I said to Albert, "Why don't I know what to do with that

67

piece of wood? I never learned anything. Why don't I know what a marking-out gauge is?"

"It's in the drawer," my father said.

Albert adjusted the gauge and scored the top of the piece of wood.

"And where's the rip saw?" he asked.

I gave it to him.

Albert began to saw down into the top of the wood.

From upstairs, my mother called, "Jim." Her voice sounded small.

Albert put down the saw.

"What is it?" my father asked.

"Ma's calling."

"Calling me?"

"I'll go see what she wants."

"Is she calling me?"

"I'll go see. I'll be right back." Albert said to me, "You continue."

"I'm not sure what to do."

"Ask Père. Try to get him to use his mind. It'll do him a lot of good to use his mind."

"Dad," I said in a louder voice, "what am I to do with this?"

"Help him, Dad," Albert said. "He wants to learn."

"Jim, Jim," my mother called.

Albert hurried away.

"You've got to make a tenon at the end of that piece," my father said.

"What's a tenon?"

"If you do what I say, you'll see what a tenon is."

Instructed by my father, I cut the tenon using the rip saw, then the tenon saw. Albert did not come back down. I cut tenons in more pieces of wood. Then my father taught me to mark out the mortise and use the brace and bit to drill into it, and the mallet and mortise chisel to cut it out. As he watched me, my father kept his hand on the piece of wood into which I was cutting the mortise, and each time I struck the chisel my father's hand jumped a little; it was as if he were holding it in place in the vise.

Albert came back.

"How is she?" my father asked.

"She's all right."

"What did she want?"

"Just to know what we were doing."

My father blinked rapidly. "I think I'll go up to her."

"Stay with us, Père," Albert said. "Stay and tell us what to do."

Albert cut a second mortise into the piece of wood. The chips flew out when, from time to time, he blew hard into the cut. He worked quickly and neatly, and the mortise he made was clean and sharp-edged, while mine was splintered and a little uneven.

"We'll get it finished quickly," I said to my father.

He shook his head a little.

"It'll take days," Albert said.

"Days?"

I want to leave, but I must stay, I thought; I must.

At angles to one another on the grey-pink carpet of the living room were the heavy chairs and sofa, and, among them, Albert and I placed the table. It was low and wide, with thick legs, and the dark-grained wood was glossily varnished.

Edmond said, "How about that. That's really something. That really is a beautiful table. That's something."

No one else spoke.

"Wait," Edmond said. "I'm going to take a picture. Wait where you are." He went into his room and, his fat body shaking, came back quickly with a flash camera. "All of you get together around the table." He peered through the camera. "Come on, Ma, get in closer to Dad. And smile. All of you smile." There was a flash.

Albert looked at his watch. "I guess I'd better get ready to go to Mass," he said.

"I will, too," I said.

In my room, I put on a tie, then sat on the edge of the bed.

I thought: London—

My mother pushed the door slowly open and entered. "Daniel," she said.

"I'm here," I said.

"Where?"

I got up and went to her; she grasped my arm.

She whispered, "I want to talk to you. I can talk to you, can't I?"

"Yes."

"I've always been able to talk to you. Even when you're not here, I talk to you, and I imagine you hear me."

"I do hear you."

She searched the air about my face. "I wanted to talk to you about the table. Is the door closed?"

"It's open."

"Close it, will you?"

I closed it and returned to her. She was in her blue house-coat; some of the safety pins were open.

"What do you think of it?" she asked.

"The table?"

She made a face. Her nose became long. "I don't like it, do you?"

"You don't?"

"No. I think it's ugly."

I put my arms around her and laughed. "It is," I said.

She laughed. "Sh," she said.

"Oh, Momma," I said.

"Sh. He'll hear us laughing."

I bit my lower lip.

"I know it's well made," my mother said, "like this house is well made, but, well, that's it, the house is ugly, the table is ugly."

"I didn't know what to do," I said, "but just follow what he said to do."

"What will Philip make of it?" She shrugged her narrow, hunched shoulders. "It's Philip's, he'll take it away, that's it, well, will he keep it in his house?"

"That'll be up to Philip."

"It's enough, I know, that is, that your father made it, if it pleases your father, that's enough, it pleases me, it should, well, please us all."

"Yes."

"But it is ugly."

Edmond came in. "What're you laughing about in here? What are you two up to?"

My mother said to me, "You won't tell your father you think it's ugly, will you? You'll let him think you think it's beautiful, won't you?"

"Of course, Momma."

"The table?" Edmond asked. "That's a beautiful table Père made."

I said, "That's what we were saying."

My mother reached for and squeezed my hand.

At Mass, I thought of the table. It became large, and appeared to float over the congregation.

In the car, I said to Albert, "I was thinking of Dad at Mass."

Whenever I was with Albert, I searched for a generalization. It seemed to me that Albert was not interested in particulars, that he found no moral in particulars. With anyone else—with anyone apart from my family—I was embarrassed to make generalizations, though I wanted to, and I made them secretly to myself. In my family, to make a generalization was to be moral and serious. I loved this overriding sense of the serious in my family.

"Yes?" Albert asked.

But I couldn't say.

Philip and Jenny, in their coats, were in the living room, examining the table. Philip was crouching. My father and mother were standing together, and behind them was Edmond with his camera raised.

Philip stood and said to Albert and me as we entered, "You've done a lot of work."

"Not really," Albert said.

"We did what Dad told us to do," I said. "The work is really all his."

"It's good work," Philip said, his intelligent voice low and sad. He looked at the table. His voice went lower. "Good work."

Edmond said to them, "It'll look beautiful in your home, it will."

"Yes," Jenny said softly.

"Will you take it today?" my mother asked.

"It won't fit into the car," Philip said. "We'll have to come another time with a van."

"When?"

"It looks lovely here," Jenny said.

"Well," Philip said, raising his voice, "you did it, Dad, you did it."

My father frowned; his chest rose and fell with his quick breathing.

Turning to him, my mother looked at him, and I saw pain come slowly into her eyes. "Jim," she called.

"Yes," he said. He had phlegm in his throat; he tried to clear it.

"It is a beautiful table," she said.

He shrugged. He smiled.

"It is," she said.

"Now I can die," he said.

Her voice jumped. "No, no. Don't say that. Don't."

He kept smiling.

Albert said, "I've got to pick up Aunt Claire at the Cathedral. She's bringing communion to Père and Mère."

My mother continued to stare at my father, who stood at the edge of the carpet and stared out.

"Come and see the photographs I took of Antonia's graduation," Edmond said to Philip and Jenny. "They didn't all come out, but a lot did. Antonia looks beautiful in her cap and gown." He held up his hands. "Really beautiful."

"Come with us, Père," Philip said to his father.

My mother said, quietly, to Philip, "Let him be."

"You don't want me to stay and—?"

Albert said, "It's best to let them be."

"Let us be," my mother said.

We left my father and mother in the living room. While, in his bedroom, Edmond showed Philip and Jenny the photographs, I walked back and forth across the kitchen floor. Passing the door to the living room, I looked in; I saw, standing still in the lines of fine light through the dimness, as in a room of their own, my mother and father, she at the far end and he at the side. My mother went to him, and she put her arms around him and leaned her forehead against his jaw.

I went into my bedroom and stood at the window to look out at the bright sunlight on the hedge along the narrow yard.

When I heard the back entry door open, I went out, my Aunt Claire came in silently, with her purse held close to her bosom. She smiled at Edmond, at Philip and Jenny, at me as

73

we came out to meet her, but we stayed away from her, and didn't speak to her.

Albert took her coat and preceded her into the living room. On a small bookcase of encyclopaedias was a crucifix and a candle; he lit the candle. My parents were sitting motionless in chairs. Aunt Claire opened her purse, took out a round gold pyx, and put the purse on an empty chair; as she went to my parents, smiling, she opened the pyx to reveal the white host. Jenny stood in the doorway, her head lowered; we brothers knelt.

Raising the host above the pyx, my aunt said, in a subdued voice, "Voici l'Agneau de Dieu, voici celui qui efface les péchés du monde."

As my aunt broke the host and fed sections to my father and mother, I looked out through a slat lifted on one blind to the sunlit street, where a man was walking slowly past the house.

I thought: My father, my father and my mother are taken up into the Body of Christ, the Body which includes, a great generalization, everything, the entire world, and everything in the world.

I followed Aunt Claire, my mother's younger and only surviving sister, into the pantry, where, at the sink, she filled the shallow pyx with water, said a silent prayer, and drank the water before she turned to me and kissed me on my cheek.

"How's it been?" she asked.

"All right."

"How much longer you going to stay?"

"I'm going off later today to visit Richard and André. I want to see all my brothers before I return to London."

"You want to get back to London?"

"I do, yes."

"It's been tough here, hasn't it? It hasn't really been all right."

"It hasn't been easy."

74

"You know, Dan, I don't know what's to be done for your father. I've tried and tried to help. Finally, all I could think of was to ask at the Cathedral for special permission to take him and your mother the sacrament. I couldn't think of anything more. If I didn't come, he'd never receive. I don't think he'd care. He wouldn't do anything. You'd think he didn't have a religion."

"Yes."

"I ask myself, What sustains him? And I can't answer."

"Yes," I said, "I know."

"When he was bringing up the family, working hard, he knew what he had to do, what his duty was, because he didn't have a choice, but now—" She held up her hands; the pyx was in one. "His world has no outside."

After I packed, I sat by my father, he in his rocking chair by the kitchen window. His breathing was reedy; he didn't speak, and I didn't speak.

Then he said, in French, "Is it difficult to write a book?"

A little surprised by his French, I answered in French, "I find it difficult."

"I read, years ago, books by Benjamin Constant and Prosper Mérimée. And who wrote *L'Abbé Constantin?*"

"I don't know."

"You don't?"

"I should. But I don't."

He went silent.

"Did you like *L'Abbé Constantin?*" I asked.

"I hardly remember. It was very well written. The language was beautiful. I remember that. I remember, too, it was set in a village in France."

"Do you know where in France your French ancestors came from before they went to Canada?"

75

"I don't know, no. But I like *L'Abbé Constantin*. We read it, I think, at the parish school. You should try to read it if you can get it."

"I will."

Yet again, he fell silent; he appeared to think and lose his thoughts. He asked, "What makes writing difficult?"

He still spoke in French, perhaps not quite knowing what language he was using.

I leaned towards him. "The greatest difficulty for me?" I said.

"Yes." He listened.

I had to think the sentence out in French before I said, "To write, not about what I feel and think, but what someone else does."

"That is difficult?"

"Yes. Because I can't do it, I think I should stop."

"Do you always write in English?"

"I don't think I could write in French."

"You've forgotten?"

I said in English, "I was trying to recall, the other day, the word for file, and I couldn't."

"Why is it difficult to write, not about yourself, but someone other?"

My brother Albert came into the kitchen. He said, "I thought I should tell you, Daniel, that if you want to catch that train, you should get started."

In the living room, my mother was sitting in a big chair; the room was darkened, and she wore dark spectacles. I kissed her.

"You'll be back soon?" she asked.

"I will."

"I know you have to go."

I kissed her again.

Albert was waiting for me in the kitchen with my suitcase

and my jacket. I put on the jacket and went to my father. My hands on his shoulders, I bent over and kissed him on his cheeks.

As I drew back, he was pointing at me.

He said, "I want to tell you—"

"What is it, Père?"

"Work hard," he said.

"I'll try."

"And be a good boy."

PART TWO

THERE WAS A large door, painted white, at the end of the room, open to a screen door; beyond the screen, blurred, were the woods. On the leaf-covered lawn outside the door lay bare broken branches among the red lawn furniture. The air was humid and warm. Smooth-skinned and slightly plump, my mother stood at the screen door and looked out. Her brown hair was waved at her forehead; in the waves were streaks of grey. She had a rosary wound round her left wrist.

Edmond, thin, came into the living room from the kitchen.

My mother turned to him. "It's you," she said.

"Who'd you think it'd be?" he asked.

"I thought it might be your father."

"I'm going out in my boat alone," Edmond said, "before anybody gets here and asks me for a ride. I told Billy I'd be around, and he'll be waiting for me on his wharf."

"Who's Billy?" my mother asked.

Edmond's eyes opened large. "He's the son of these people, there, who just this year bought the house beyond the island, there."

"How old is Billy?"

"He's thirteen."

"And you're almost thirty. Do his parents know you take him out for rides in your boat?"

Edmond's eyes opened wider. "Sure they do, sure, I know

his parents, there, they treat me like I'm an older brother of Billy—"

"Where is your father?" my mother asked.

My father came in to the living room from the dining room. He was wearing a white T-shirt, and his arms and chest expanded the shirt. He was carrying a hammer. He said to my mother, "I was looking for you."

Edmond opened the screen door and left.

"I was here," my mother said.

"I don't know what we're going to do," my father said. "The storm knocked out the electricity, the pump, the electric stove, the fridge. The lights don't work. What're we going to do when the house is full?"

My mother said, "What should we do?"

My father winced.

"I know it's difficult for you to have all your sons around you now. But they bought you this house because you lost your job, you know, and they want to be with you in it. Don't you see they bought it for you so that you'd have—?" She stopped to look past him and through the screen door. Richard was standing among the broken branches.

My mother went to the doorway. She called, "Richard."

She stepped back as Richard came in, scratching the backs of his hands. He was almost bald. He smiled at my parents and said, softly, "I was just relaxing before everyone gets here."

My mother said, "Your father thinks it's a bad idea, all of us getting together this weekend. He says it's because we don't have any electricity."

My father looked at my mother; his fixed wince made him look as if he had smelled a very bad smell which he couldn't locate.

Richard said, more softly, "Gee, Dad, I think we can manage."

82

My father said to my mother, "You should rest."

Putting his hand on her shoulder, Richard said, "She's all right, Dad."

"I've got to replace a few shingles that blew off the roof," my father said.

"Don't go out on the roof," my mother said.

"I can get through a gable window, don't worry."

"I wish you wouldn't."

"I'll go out for you, Dad," Richard said.

"No, I'll do it. This house was given to me by my sons. I want to maintain it in good reparation."

Richard started after him.

"Let him go," my mother said. "It'll give him something to do. He can't be idle. He always needs something to do, and when he doesn't have anything he occupies himself taking care of me."

Richard laughed. "You sound as if you don't mind getting rid of him for half an hour, Ma."

My mother's eyes widened. "Oh no. No. I didn't mean that. I meant he'd be getting a rest from me by doing a little work."

But she and Richard exchanged long looks. Richard said, "Well, there've been times when I didn't mind a half-hour away from Dad." He reached out, hugged her, and said, "Oh Ma." She laughed. He let her go.

She said, "I'll bet you miss your wife and kids."

"Yes, yes," he said.

She reached out and touched his wrist. "I understand."

"I wonder sometimes what's wrong in my family," he said. "I do what I think is right. Chuckie does what she thinks is right. We both do. On the whole, you know, we don't disagree. But it's as though something is wrong, outside our control. If we knew what is wrong, we'd put it right. The kids really get out of control. We don't know what to do." He

83

scratched his hands. He stared at his mother, and as he did his eyes appeared to go a little out of focus. "Sometimes," he said, "I wish someone would tell me."

My mother said, "Your eczema's bad again."

He held out the backs of his hands.

She said, "I can't tell you."

"But how did you do it?"

"I don't know." She frowned. "I don't know, Richard."

He smiled. "Don't worry, Ma, don't worry about me or my family; everything will be all right, I promise."

"Yes."

My mother stood in the middle of the room. Richard went to the screen door to look out. At the edge of the lawn was a low stone wall against which was a drift of grey-brown leaves, and beyond the wall was the dirt drive sloping down and round to the lake. Halfway down the drive was a fallen pine tree. Julien and I, in bathing suits, were sawing, on either side of a two-handed saw, the branches from the tree. We were sweating. By the tree was a heap of pine branches. André came up the drive and, his hands on his hips, stood near us to watch us.

Richard turned back to my mother. She had closed her eyes.

"Ma," he said.

She opened her eyes.

"Are you all right?"

She pressed the middle of her forehead. "If you knew the effort I'm making and will make, not only for your father, but for the boys, and all the efforts of will I make seem to me to be—"

The screen door opened. André, in neat sports clothes, came in. He raised his hands and said in a loud voice, "Hi there." His face, with fine clear features, was tanned; his black hair was very short.

"Where've you been?" Richard asked, raising his voice. "We've been really missing you around here for the last hour."

André smiled a large white smile. "Oh, I took a walk."

"Where to?" my mother asked.

"I walked along a path in the woods until it stopped at a broken-down cabin."

"Is someone living there?"

"No, no. It was abandoned. The roof was fallen in and the windows were gone."

"I see," my mother said.

André startled her a little, so she put her arms to her breasts, by suddenly putting his arms round her and pulling her to him; she stumbled a little, and he held her up. He kissed her on the temple. "You're my girl," he said. "I wouldn't want better, you're the best, the better than best."

I, outside the screen door, shaded my eyes to see through into the living room. I asked, "Is Dad there?"

"No," Richard said.

My father answered, "Yes, I am."

Richard turned to my father, just inside the room. André quickly let go of my mother, who lurched a little.

"Dad," I said, "do you have any rope?"

"For what?"

"Jule and I have cut all the branches off the tree that fell so we've got a nice long bare trunk, and Jule wants to haul it up whole to the house by using logs as rollers and a rope to pull."

"Why does Julien want to have it up here?" Richard asked.

"You ask me why Jule does anything."

My father said, "There's a coil of rope under my work bench in the boiler room."

I left.

André said in the silence between my mother and father,

"Sometimes I wonder if I'll get married, but then I think of you two, a beaming example to us all, and I know I will, I know I want to marry—"

I rushed up to the screen door, pulled it open, and announced, "Albert's come."

Everyone in the room went still.

"Where is he?" my mother asked.

"He's been talking to Jule down by the tree about how to haul it up to the house. The taxi couldn't get further."

My mother took a step forward.

Outside, through the grey air, came Albert, carrying a small case; he was dressed in a tan suit, and his shoes were highly polished.

I held the screen door open for Albert to enter, but stayed outside. As my father drew back my mother rushed forward to put her arms around Albert, who, his case in one hand, embraced her with his left arm.

He said, soberly, "It's a pleasure to have you greet me like this, Ma."

She stepped back and he, bending only his knees, put his bag down.

"You see," she said, "you see—" But she couldn't say.

"Come on now, Mom," Albert said.

She embraced him again and he put both his large brown hands on her small back; he kept his neck rigid, his chin in, as if his face were at attention.

She let him go and stepped back. She touched her eyes with the tips of her fingers. "No," she said, "no tears, I'm not crying, I'm so happy you've come, and, believe me, this time you'll be happy, too, to be here, it won't be like last time, no moaning and groaning."

Albert crossed the room to my father, who expanded his chest. They shook hands sombrely.

"How are you?" Albert asked.

86

"Well, I don't know how we're all going to stay in the house, it has no electricity, and no facilities because of that."

My mother said from the other end of the long room, "Everything is going to be all right. Philip and his wife will be coming. Soon we'll all be together. Everything is going to be, I know everything is going to be"—she raised her hands—"just wonderful."

Her husband and her two eldest sons stared at her.

She said, "We'll have some tea now, iced tea, how about that, iced tea?"

André said, "I'll make it. But first—" With a little jump he went to Albert and silently they shook hands.

Richard stood apart, scratching his hands. He was older than Albert, the eldest of the seven sons.

My mother said, "And now we'll all sit down for some iced tea."

André went into the kitchen. Albert took off his jacket, under which he wore a white short-sleeved shirt; he loosened his tie and unbuttoned his collar. He sat on the couch, my father in the platform rocker, my mother on a straight-back chair, and Richard remained standing back.

"Well," my father said, rising, "I've got some work to do on the house still."

"Not now, Jim," my mother said.

"I want the house to be kept in good reparation."

"It looks all right to me," Albert said.

My father said, "I worked hard to buy this house. I want to keep it in good reparation."

Everyone went silent.

Albert said, "Don't think of the family, Dad, think of yourself and Mom, this is your house. And if it gets too much for you, keeping it in repair, sell it and use the money in whatever way you want."

"I'll go see to a broken window pane," my father said. He went out.

"He's got to be doing something," my mother said, "so he thinks his job is to keep up this house."

Albert said, "But he doesn't really like this house, does he?"

"Oh, he does."

"He'd much rather be in his house in the city."

From the kitchen André entered with a red tin tray on which were glasses of iced tea. He held the tray out first to his mother, and he seemed not to know if he should then offer it to Richard or Albert, but Richard stood further back and held his hand out to Albert, and André lowered the tray before his second oldest brother, the Marine major. André put the tray on the low table before the couch and took a glass, and Richard came himself for a glass with yellow flowers on it. They sipped.

My mother said, "Why, Albert, did your father say he bought this house for the family when he knows you all bought it for him?"

Albert snapped, "Ma."

She looked at him. She tilted her head. She said, "Without a job, he feels he has nothing." She leaned far over and placed the glass, from which she had taken a sip, on the low table, and she sat back, straight, silent.

Albert said to André, "Have you been painting any more paintings, kid?"

"Oh yes," André said. "At sea I did. I painted one of a sunset."

"I'd like to see it," Albert said.

André stretched his neck by twisting his head from side to side, then he glanced at my mother, who sat rigid, and he said, "I'll show you some day."

Richard said, laughing a little, "Hey, I've got a joke."

"Have you ever thought, lad, where your gift comes from?" Albert asked André.

My mother said to Richard, "Well, what's your joke?"

"I have thought," André said, "and I don't know where it comes from."

Richard lowered his eyes, but looked quickly at everyone in the room, smiling. "It's about—" he said. He laughed. His front teeth were large, with a space between them. "It's about this guy who's got to go to the toilet real bad—"

Albert said, "I brought a gift for the family." By the door, he opened his case and from it took, wrapped in layers of tissue, a package which he stood upright on the floor, and, crouching, he tore the layers of tissue away to a clock in a gleaming dome. He lifted the dome and wound the clock; all the golden gears and springs showed behind the round white face. At the base of the clock were four golden balls which started going, round in one direction, then back round in the opposite direction, back and forth.

My mother got up to look at the clock. She said, "It's beautiful."

The four golden balls moved round, back round, back round.

Richard said, "I didn't bring a present. I guess I'm not very thoughtful."

My mother watching him closely, Albert picked up the clock and put it on the coffee table, and they both turned away from it.

My mother said, "You should've used the money you spent on that on yourself, Albert. We don't need—"

On the lawn, Julien, in a black bathing suit, was pulling at a rope tied round the tree trunk, about ten feet long, under the top end of which I, running from back end to top end, placed small logs I picked up as they rolled out from under the back end. The trunk advanced on to the overgrown lawn.

Albert said, "Julien's done it."

Inside, they watched the big pine trunk stop among the lawn furniture. Julien dropped the rope and I, bent over with a log in my hand, stood up and threw the log down.

My mother said, "That tree trunk will lie there till it rots."

Albert said, "I'm going to get changed."

"I think I'll go to my room and lie down a little," Richard said, and he went out before his brother.

My mother stopped Albert. "I wonder if we should go to the house in the city, your father and I, and leave you boys to take care of yourselves here."

"Why?"

"Because you'd have a better time without your father and me."

"Come on, Ma."

She threw her shoulders back and took a deep breath. "Yes, yes," she said, "I won't forget, I promise, it'll be wonderful, our being all together, all of us." She frowned. She said, "I hope Philip and Jenny aren't staying away because they got worried that it wouldn't be all right, that your father's having been fired would—"

"They'll come."

"Maybe it'd be best if they didn't."

The right side of Albert's mouth rose into his cheek, so his eyes narrowed, and he said, as with a crack of his voice, "Ma."

She was a little startled. "Oh no, no," she said. "I want them to come, I do, I promise everything is going to be all right."

He kept his face twisted for a moment, his teeth exposed.

"I promise, I promise," she said.

His face became stark.

She touched Albert's arm, but quickly withdrew her hand. "I want everything to be all right, I really do."

He smiled; his crooked teeth showed. "I know you do."

"And you," she said, "are you all right?"

"Why are you asking?" he said.

"I thought you looked worried."

"No, not worried."

"You know, I can't imagine your life in the military, as I can't imagine anything that happens in the country."

"What don't you understand?"

"I don't want to understand, I guess."

"It's a low, filthy place, the country," Albert said, "not anything to want to know. If I thought I were defending this country and not some other country—" He stopped.

"What's wrong? I know there's something wrong. I won't understand it probably."

Albert laughed lightly.

"I so much want you all to be happy," she said.

"I wish it were up to your wishing it." He stopped again for a moment. He said, "I believe in certain high principles, Ma, I believe in them strongly, principles which exist above me and you and the whole country that I and you and the country must abide by no matter what we think or feel, and those principles make up for me another country—"

"You're strong."

"No, I'm not, I'm weak, but I fight."

She held his arm.

"Pray for me, will you?" he asked.

"Oh yes," she said, "I pray."

"I think you should go upstairs and rest," Albert said.

"Your father is always saying I should rest."

In the hall, they met my father who was coming out of the bathroom.

My mother said to him, "I'm going to go rest."

"Yes," my father said.

He watched her climb the stairs.

91

Albert remained with him, and said, "Look, Dad, I hope you're not worried about not working."

"I think," my father said, "I'll go with your mother."

Albert stood in the way. "Dad, everything will be all right."

"I hope so."

"Philip will be here soon, with Jenny. We'll all be together, the whole family."

My father twisted up his face. "But what are we going to do without facilities? We have to flush the toilet with buckets of lake water."

Calmly, Albert said, "You don't want the family together again, do you, Dad?"

His strong eyebrows raised, my father said, "Oh no, I do." His eyebrows lowered. He said, "My will has been broken, I'll do anything, I'll do anything for your mother."

"And for your sons?"

"My sons have wills of their own."

My father went upstairs and Albert returned to the dim living room where Julien and I were drinking glasses of the remaining iced tea. We were in our bathing suits.

Albert said to Julien, "You did a good job."

I said, "Al—"

"What is it, lad?"

"I wanted to ask you something," I said.

"Any time—"

Richard came into the room, and Albert turned to him. The two eldest brothers looked at one another, then Richard smiled and held out both hands. He said, "I haven't said hello yet." Albert went to him. They clutched one another's elbows, and Richard, smiling more, shook Albert until he, too, smiled. "It's good to see you," Richard said sadly. Albert disengaged himself from Richard, who immediately reached out and pulled Julien to him, hugged him, and let him go.

"You're going to be the tallest of us all," Richard said. Julien glanced at everyone, then down, and smiled.

Richard and Albert looked round to see my parents standing side by side.

My mother said, "No sign of Philip and Jenny."

"No," Albert said.

Richard said, "The storm probably—"

My mother interrupted him. "Your father thinks we can't manage it, a whole house full of people without electricity."

"It's a lot of work trying to run a house without electric power," my father said.

Richard said, "We can flush the toilet with water from the lake, take our drinking water from the well, swim to bathe, and we'll eat cold food—"

My father made a face as though he were in great pain.

All at once Albert shouted, and my parents and brother jumped. "What is this? What is this?"

My mother moaned. "Oh no."

Albert shouted from the twisted side of his mouth, "If you want to go to the house in the city, Dad, just say so, and we'll go. I won't put up with any wrangling, I won't, so just come out with it, man, come out with it, we either stay here or we go, every one of us, down to stay in the house in Providence."

My father looked down.

"That's such a small house," my mother said.

My father said, "Your mother and I will go, you boys can manage here."

Albert stuck out his jaw and his neck tendons showed. "If you go, we all go, and when I say that I mean it."

My father's eyes flickered over him and he said dimly, "I think your mother and I should go."

Albert gave the order. "All right, that's it, we're going down to the city."

93

My mother sat on a chair. She put her hands between her knees and keened a little.

"None of that, Ma," Albert said. "Get ready to go. We're going to do what Dad wants."

My mother remained sitting on the wooden chair, but motionless, and no one else moved.

I came into the room from the porch with a large red and yellow maple leaf.

André said to me, "We're going back to the city."

I said, 'Oh." I brought the leaf to my mother. "I found this," I said.

She took it and looked at it. She rocked her body back and forth. And then suddenly she stopped. She said, looking at the leaf, "Anyone'd think I want to dance."

Edmond, his hair blown about, his eyes wide, entered from outside. He carried a cap with a long visor. He asked, "What's this?"

Albert said, "We're all moving down to the city."

Edmond threw the cap on the floor. "I knew it," he said. He sat down and crossed his arms. "I knew everything was going to go wrong. I went to pick up Billy on his wharf, he said he couldn't come on a boat ride with me, his mother and father wouldn't let him."

"He's only a boy," André said.

Edmond kicked a heel against the bottom of the couch.

"If his parents knew how good you are they'd approve," Richard said.

"I'm not good," Edmond said.

My mother put her hands to her face. My father stood over her. He gently put a hand under her elbow and she rose from her chair.

Edmond said, "I'll have to go with them, I suppose."

"I'll go, Ed," Richard said.

My father said, "I can still drive. I'll go with your

94

mother." He kept his hand under her arm as they went out.

Albert said, "It'll be dark soon."

I lay full length on the couch.

Albert said to me, "We've got to get ready to go, lad."

I rose on my elbows. "Yes."

"What is it?"

"I don't want to go back to that house."

Albert asked, "What is it that you want to say to me, lad?"

I looked into the grey dimness.

There was a distant chug-chug-chug from the cellar.

Richard came in. He said, "The pump has started to work, the electricity has come on." He went about the dark room turning on lamps.

"Where are Mom and Dad?" Albert asked.

"They've already gone."

In the morning light, I was carving, with a chisel and a mallet, a face on the top of the stripped pine trunk, which lay, like a long thin yellow-pink body with its arms close to its sides, across two trestles.

Richard emerged from the woods. On the way to the house he stopped to look at my work. I drew back to examine with him the head with its long flat nose, round cheeks, bulging eyes, and chopped, mouthless jaw; there was a crack down one side of the face and resin oozed from it. Richard said to me, "That's great, Dan, really great," and I smiled and went back to the pole; I straddled it to continue carving the chin. Richard crossed the lawn to the screen door, and he entered the living room.

Albert, walking up and down the room, was saying his rosary; when he saw Richard he put the rosary into a trouser pocket.

Richard said, "I've been for a walk in the woods with Julien."

Albert smiled. "Where is he?"

"He stayed in the woods. I had to find my way back on my own."

My brother Philip went into the room. He was finely thin, his black hair combed close to his head. He carried a gigantic bright pink ear which he propped on a chair by the fireplace. Behind him was Jenny, hugely pregnant, a red and blue silk scarf knotted loosely about her neck.

"So you came," Richard said. He shook his brother's hand and hugged his sister-in-law.

Philip frowned. He said, "If it wasn't for Jenny's insisting—"

As if it were the echo of a strong, far-off voice, there came, from upstairs, the sound of André singing. Everyone listened.

Outside, I put the mallet and wood chisel on the face I was carving when I saw, coming up the dirt drive, my parents, and I went towards them; Albert rushed out of the house to meet them.

Philip said to Jenny, "Go into the kitchen, Jen."

She went.

Philip saw my mother appear, held on one side by Albert and on the other by my father, on the lawn; I was behind and I dropped back to remain outside as the three advanced into the house and stood just inside the doorway. My mother, between her son and her husband, looked down. Philip went to her. He kissed her on the side of her head. He said, "Momma." He shook my father's hand and said, as if simply stating, "Dad."

Upstairs, André continued to sing.

My mother wandered about the room, silent; she kept stopping and going in different directions. The others watched her. She stopped by a chair, held its back; she stood still, and then, about to turn away, she turned the opposite way, towards Philip, and said, "But where is your wife?"

Philip said, "Jenny."

His wife stood at the doorway to the kitchen. She held her bulging stomach. She smiled at her mother-in-law, who stared at her in silence for a moment, as in wonder, then she went to her and clutched her arms.

My mother said to my father, "Jim, Jim, another baby in the family. Come and greet your daughter-in-law."

He shook her hand. He said, "You're welcome."

Jenny said shyly, "I'm so glad."

My father crossed his arms.

"And how are your parents, so far away from you?" my mother asked.

Jenny smiled at her.

"But you've got to rest," my mother said; "I know what it's like to be expecting, I know, and I'm going to take you to your room where you can lie down and rest."

"I'm all right," Jenny said.

"Momma," Philip said.

She didn't respond; she put her arm in Jenny's to take her out, saying, "You've got to take care of yourself."

Above, André sang out, sang out and out, and then, suddenly, the singing ceased.

My father was left with his back towards his sons.

Richard held out a finger to the huge pink ear on the chair. "What's that, Phil?" he asked. "It looks like an ear big enough to hear what nobody can hear."

Philip picked up the ear and held it to his chest. He said, "Dad."

My father turned.

"I thought you might be interested," Philip said.

My father studied him.

97

Philip said, "Well, you see, what I'm trying to find out is whether our ability to tell where a sound is coming from is determined by the inner ear or the complicated structure of the outer ear."

"Yes, I understand," my father said flatly.

"I thought you might want to see how it works."

He held out the ear to my father, who silently took it.

"Now," Philip said, "put it up to one ear and block the other with a hand, then close your eyes and tell me where you think I am."

My father put the ear, in which there was a hole, to his right ear, shut his eyes and blocked his left ear.

Philip moved about quietly, and, stopping, said, softly, "Hello."

"You're off to my left," my father said.

"You're right." Philip again moved, then said, "Oh."

"To my right."

"Yes," Philip said.

My father opened his eyes and handed the ear back to Philip.

Richard said, "Now that's interesting, isn't it, Dad?"

"Yes," he said.

André, walking as with his body held high, came in and smiled at everyone; but he said nothing, and went to the door to look out at the woods.

While Albert examined the ear, Richard approached André. He asked, "Are you all right?"

André said brightly, "Of course, of course, sure I am."

"I hope we are," Richard said, "all of us, including Dad. Though I guess he never asked himself if he was all right. He did what he thought he had to do."

André said, "Even to losing everything."

Albert, holding the ear, said, "So this is what serious scientific research is all about."

"I'll tell you," Philip said, "work at its best is not serious, but a game."

My father rubbed his chin.

"You've got to enjoy it," Philip said.

André turned to them. "Yes, you've got to, you've got to enjoy it." He laughed. "But a little bit of money now and then matters, a little bit of money for the game you play."

Richard said, "We're poor, we'll always be poor, and the poor have to work without enjoying it."

Philip said to my father, "Well, Dad, you know what I mean."

My father stared at him.

Philip went to the window. He asked, "What's Dan doing?"

My father said starkly, "He's carving a pole," and he came outside to me. He stood, his hands on his hips, to watch me, straddling the pole and leaning close to carve an upper lip. I dismounted and handed the mallet and wood chisel to my father, who took my place, and, keeping his back straight, he whacked away matter-of-factly at the lip. The chips jumped. Under his shirt his muscles moved, though his body remained still; he clenched his lower teeth over his upper, so his jaw stuck out; his eyes were bright black. One by one, Richard and André and Albert came out to see him carve.

Alone in the living room, Philip asked Jenny, "Are you all right?"

"It is a little strange," she said.

"Of course it is for you."

"Every time I look at your father I imagine he thinks I'm too foreign to be comprehensible to him in any way."

Through the window, Philip saw Richard go into the woods.

"To my father there is only his tribe," he said. "I want you

99

to stand apart, as I want to stand apart. We won't come often, don't worry, we'll lead our own lives together."

As if she had been walking about the house and did not know where to settle, my mother came into the room. She saw Jenny and said, "Oh, you're up."

"I did have a rest," Jenny said.

My mother looked carefully at her. She said, "You're in the family now."

Jenny blinked rapidly.

Philip said, "We're going out for a walk, Momma."

My mother looked past them out of the window, and, her eyes wide in the livid light, she stared into the grey, gaunt woods. Her brows and forehead rose as her eyes widened a little more.

Philip glanced around.

Jenny said gently to her mother-in-law, "Why don't you come with us?"

My mother looked through her. It took her a moment to say, softly, "No, no," and, as if all the energy had gone from her, she again said, "No," and turned away as they went. She walked about the room, lightly knocking her fists against the backs of chairs. She looked towards the window and again she stared out into the woods.

Outside, Philip shouted. Albert ran off. My father stopped chiselling the face to look up. Jenny, limping a little, came supported by Philip and Albert, Richard closely following. She was laughing and saying, "But I'll be all right, I am all right." My mother, still, faced Jenny as she came into the house. My father, the last in, went to my mother.

I straddled the pole and continued to carve an eye.

Jenny's face was flushed. She said, "I just fell to my knees." But her face went dark and she placed her hands on her stomach.

My mother took a step towards her, then stopped.

Jenny slowly smiled; she lowered her hands from her stomach.

My mother's lips twisted, and she said, trying to smile, "I hope it'll be a boy," and a sob broke from her which surprised her and made her lose her breath, so she put her hand to her heart; after a moment, her eyes wide, she laughed and looked at her family.

In the silence, Richard came up to her, and she, holding his head, kissed him on the cheek. He went outside. She took a step towards Albert, who quickly came towards her, and she kissed him on his lowered forehead, and he gravely went outside. She looked about; her blue eyes staring, she seemed to have difficulty seeing. She turned to Philip, standing next to Jenny, and as she raised her hands to him he raised his, held her shoulders, and kissed her on the side of her neck, under her ear. She turned away from him, searching, as if she had never seen it before, the room; André strode to her, his arms wide, and he clasped her in them and pulled her so tightly against him she leaned a little away from him to breathe. Philip and Jenny went out. André leaned over his mother and kissed her on both temples. She laughed. When he let her go suddenly to go out, too, she lost her balance and my father, by her, had to hold her elbow to steady her. My mother, alone with him, hugged my father close. He held her. She drew back to look at him, or, her pupils expanding and contracting as with the effort to focus, she tried to look at him, smiling; she grasped his hands and gently lifted them from her, and said, "Go out and join the others," and he left her.

She heard Julien, far off, call, and she stopped to listen, but she couldn't make out the call.

At the window in the living room she saw Edmond, carrying an inflated inner tube, go into the bare woods, where her other sons and her daughter-in-law were standing, and her husband half hidden by a pine tree.

PART THREE

I

IN THE CROWD outside the Boston airport, my brother
Philip was waiting for me. I put down my case. When we
embraced, our breaths heaved. Then, stepping back, Philip
said, "Let me take your bag." We walked out of the terminal
in silence, and across the wind-blown parking lot to the car.
The thin yellow, late winter light floated above the dark
ground, and we drove through it.

"How is Momma?" I asked.

"I honestly don't know," Philip said. "I haven't yet been
down to the house."

I looked out of the window at the flat light, rising higher
from the darkening highways and bare woods outside
Boston.

"How is Jenny?" I asked.

"She's well."

"And your family?"

"The kids are living away from home now. Antonia came
back last night, and the others will come in tomorrow."

"All of us sons will be there?"

"They're waiting for you and me to make it all of us."

I said, "When Albert rang me, he said, 'We know it's far
for you to come, we don't expect—'"

"How is London?" Philip asked.

"It hardly seems to exist now."

We drove past woods with clapboard houses, and the high, greying light, level, through the trees.

I said, "How beautiful it is here."

"I guess we take it for granted," Philip said.

"I've lived away for, now, going on twenty years."

"So long?"

"It seems strange to me."

"Why?"

"I'm not sure. The country seems strange to me."

Philip drove to a large brown house, with many high gables, in the woods.

His wife Jenny made tea, and we sat at the dining-room table, covered with a lace cloth, and drank the tea from fine white cups.

It is strange, I thought.

I asked, "Do you mind if I take a little walk before we go to Providence?"

"Sure thing, Dan," Philip said.

The air was cold and clear. I went out into the woods, my overcoat over my shoulders. I breathed in the air, which had a faint smell of mould; I breathed it in more deeply for the smell as I walked on, among the trees. The branches rose into the remaining light; at the level of the light was wind, and the branches moved in it, while below there was calm. My shoes sank into the mould of old wet leaves. I came out to a clearing where, at the centre, logs were piled in cords, stakes on either side to hold the cords up. In the gloaming, they were, these squared stacks, like the small huts of a settlement amid tree stumps and mist rising in the woods. I walked round the clearing, then back to the house, where the light above the front door was lit.

We drove down to Providence in the dark.

I asked, "What did Dad die of?"

"I don't really know," Philip said. "His body just gave in."

"I see."

"Albert will know. He's taken over, made all the arrangements. He was with Dad when he died."

"And Momma?"

"Momma was with him too."

"Not Edmond?"

"No. Edmond was at work. But this is big drama for Ed, and he'll tell you about it, dramatically, all of it."

I went ahead of the others, through the back entry into the kitchen. It was crowded with my family, some standing, some seated about the table. They all turned to me, and towards me came my oldest brother, Richard, with his hands extended. His eyes were red.

Richard put his arms about me and held me close, and when he released me he kept his hands on my shoulders and looked at me. He looked at me, his eyes blinking, as if he were trying to say something; he said, finally, "It's a pleasure to see you, Dan," and hugged me to him again. When he stepped back his eyes were wet, and he looked at me trying to speak. He said, quietly, "Ah." He shook his head and turned a little away, then turned back. His voice was soft. He said, "We're all separated, we brothers, and hardly know what one another is doing, and yet that doesn't matter, because we know one another in a bigger way, which keeps us together. Isn't that so?"

"Yes," I said.

"It keeps us knowing Dad, too," Richard said.

Everyone in the kitchen was silent.

Richard swung his hand out, slowly and gently, and hit me on my shoulder. He smiled. "It is good to see you," he said. "Why don't you come back for a long while soon and stay with us? We'd love to have you. We'd like to know what you've been up to."

"I will."

"I wish you would."

Richard and his wife Chuckie had eight children. The youngest was twenty-one. Richard was on the board of a company in western Massachusetts which manufactured industrial gauges.

I asked, "How are you all?"

Richard looked down. "Not so good, not all of us."

"I'm sorry."

"Well, well," Richard said, "well—"

I looked past him to where Albert was standing, as at attention, and I went to him; Albert held me stiffly, a little away from him, and we touched cheeks on both sides, quickly.

I said, "You've organized everything."

"No worry," Albert said. "None at all. The wake will be tomorrow, just one day, and the funeral the following morning. As I was here, I did it all easily." His voice was matter-of-fact. "There's no worry. I just had to take care of a few details, and they were no bother, no bother, they hardly count."

"No," I said.

"Just details," Albert said.

"If there is anything I can do—"

"As I said, don't worry, lad, everything's been taken care of."

"Thank you for doing that for all of us."

Albert seemed to stand again at attention, chin drawn in, his eyes fixed over my head.

My brother André, in his black Navy uniform with gold braid on the sleeves, said from across the kitchen, "You're right, Dan, you're right to thank Al for what he's done. We all owe him many thanks." He came towards me, smiling widely. "He's a great guy."

Saying nothing, Albert stepped back.

"And so are you, Dan," André said. He embraced me and patted me on the back with both hands. "So are you, old man."

"Thanks."

"It's been too long since we've seen one another," André said, drawing away to look at me. "And you're well, I can see you're very well."

"I am, yes."

"I'm so pleased."

"And you," I said, "you seem very well."

"Oh, Dan, yes, I guess I'm well."

He smiled, then, suddenly, his smile fell. I hugged him again.

André said, starkly, "Dad was a great man."

"He was, yes."

"In every way, he was great."

"Yes," I said. "Yes."

When I released him André was smiling again. "It really is good to see you," he said, "really really good."

"And you."

"Look, Antoinette and I would love to have you come and stay with us. You should know your nephews and nieces. We've been stationed abroad in difficult places for a long while, but now that we're homeside for a while, you come back home, too, and visit us."

"I will. I will."

"You know, Antoinette's father died before we were married, and she always regretted that her dad couldn't meet mine. She said to me, as I was leaving her and the kids in Washington, 'Well, now our fathers can meet.' I said, 'That's beautiful, Antoinette, that's really beautiful.'"

"It is."

"So you'll come?"

"I will."

"Your younger brother is just behind you," André said.

I turned from André to Julien standing in front of me, waiting; and before I could speak, Julien put his long powerful arms about me and hugged me close and pressed his face into my neck. I, too, held him close, and we remained still. When we separated, tears were running down our faces. Julien looked away. He left the kitchen to go into the living room.

I went to Richard's wife Chuckie, who, at the table, was quietly drinking a cup of tea and leafing through a magazine. I kissed her. Three of her children were at the table with her, and they rose. I kissed two of my nieces and shook hands with a nephew. I had not seen them since they had become adults. I said, "I wouldn't have recognized you." They laughed quietly and shifted their weight from foot to foot.

Tapped on the back, I turned to my brother Edmond. Edmond said, "My brother, my brother from a long way away." He kissed me on the cheek, near my mouth, over and over. "My brother." His body against mine was soft. "Now all my brothers are together." He wore spectacles, and tears collected at the bottoms of the rims. "Now we're all together."

"We are, we are," I said.

"And in such sadness." Edmond drew me aside, by the kitchen stove, and he said, his eyes big and staring, "But I wouldn't want him back, Dan. No, not the way he was, not the way he was suffering. He worked too hard to die."

"Where is Momma?" I asked, interrupting him.

"She's in the living room."

"I want to go see her."

Edmond put his hand on my arm to keep me. "In the end," he said, "he was very bad. He didn't know where he was. He couldn't go to the bathroom by himself. We had to feed him. We had to put him in the middle room, finally, because he was talking and shouting in his sleep and keeping Mère awake. I kept the door of the middle room open, and my door, and I'd half sleep, listening if he was all right. Just two nights ago I hear him groaning, and I get up and go into the middle room and say, 'Père, what's wrong?' and he says, 'I ache, my chest aches,' and I say, 'I'm going to call the rescue squad,' and he sits up, sits right up, and says, 'I'll be all right, help me to the bathroom,' and when I get him back into bed, he says to me, 'Don't tell the boys about the pain in my chest,' and I say, 'All right, Père, I won't.' I didn't tell Al when he came in that morning. Then, the next night, when I was putting him to bed, he says to me, 'Ed, you've been a good boy, thank you and goodbye,' and that was the last I saw of him." The tears drained from the rims of Edmond's spectacles down his cheeks. "He died the next day, with Momma and Al with him, while I was at work."

"What did he die of, Ed?"

"Oh, I don't know, Dan. I don't know what he died of."

"You did a lot for him."

"It's going to be tough now, not having him; it was tough the last months having him, and I'm glad he's not here to suffer any more, but it's going to be tough not having him."

In a corner of the kitchen, Albert was sitting in his father's rocking chair and rocking a little; near him, on kitchen chairs, were Richard and Philip, in their shirt sleeves, and André, and they were talking.

I heard André say, "It's a very complex situation there."

Albert sucked his teeth and rocked.

"That part of the world is too complex to make any clear generalization about what's to be done," André said. He pulled down the sleeves of his uniform jacket.

Albert stopped rocking. "What's complex? You take a position, and you stick to the position. That simplifies. What's wrong with our policies now is that we try too hard to understand the other guy's policies, and end up wondering if ours are right. We can't get into a defensive position towards our own. We can't do it." He slammed the palm of his hand down on the arm of the rocking chair. "We've got to take a simple, strict attitude which rises above all the complex and loose attitudes. The details don't matter."

"Well," André said quietly, "you may be right, Al, you may be right."

Richard unbuttoned the cuffs of his shirt sleeves, rolled them up and scratched the backs of his hands. He said softly, "I don't know, Al. It's our principle that a majority of the people should determine how their country is run, and so often, so very often, we support in other countries dictators who're hated by the people, and destroy the countries."

Philip said, "I think we need a strong government."

Richard said sadly, "I wonder. Strong governments can just as easily destroy as save."

Philip said, "Well, I'm not really very informed." He stood up.

"No one really is," André said. "We don't really know."

Philip smiled. "I'm going to find Momma," he said.

"Our policies—" Albert began.

"I'd like to know what you think," André said. "I really would, Al."

Richard looked away from Albert. He looked about the kitchen, then at his wife and his children at the other end of the table; his lids, his mouth, his cheeks appeared to be pulled down, but, looking at his children and his wife talking, he smiled a little against the weight.

Edmond said to me, "We're all going to miss him so much. We don't yet know how much we're going to miss him."

From the living room, my mother came into the kitchen. She stopped for a moment at the doorway to hold on to the jamb before she continued. She was bent far over, so her head, with thin grey and white hair, was lowered and twisted to the side. She had on large slippers and the old blue housecoat, the blue torn in places to the white inside padding and pinned with many safety pins. She reached out to support herself with her hand against one wall of the passage from the living room, and she shuffled very slowly out into the kitchen.

Small and bent, she seemed to me to be wandering, alone, among large people she did not know.

She shuffled, her hand out, from chair back to chair back.

With a great heave in my chest, I went to her and put my arms around her. I realized, when I held her, how twisted her body had become. She pushed against my chest to look up at me to see who was holding her.

She said, "Oh Daniel."

All my feelings went out to her.

In a flat thin voice, she said, "He's in heaven now, he's in heaven."

I felt her small body strain against my holding her, and when I let go of her she turned away from me without looking at me and continued to shuffle about the kitchen.

Stunned, I watched her.

A tall young man came out of the living room, and Edmond held out a hand to him and said to me, "This'll be a surprise for you. Look, Tommy Walters. I thought, Dan'll be surprised when he sees Tommy." Tommy shook my hand and smiled; he had large hands, and he held one of my hands in both of his. "Tommy and me," Edmond said, "we'd like to take you up to the shopping mall. Don't we want to, Tommy? Didn't we say that one day we'd take Dan to the shopping mall?" "We sure did," Tommy said. "Tommy's been helping me with my trains," Edmond said; "we're building a whole town together." "That's right," Tommy said. Edmond stood back to look at Tommy and he said to me,

113

"You haven't seen him in some time. He's seventeen now. Hasn't he changed? Don't you think he's changed a lot? He's grown up." I said, "Yes, you've grown up." Tommy, squeezing my hand, said, "I came when I heard your father died, I thought I'd come and ask if there was anything I can do." "Isn't that something?" Edmond said. I said, "Thanks, Tommy." Tommy let my hand go.

"You see," Edmond said, "he came back to his family. We're Tommy's family."

We had to separate to let my mother, shuffling towards us, pass us; she touched the stove, then turned to shuffle away from it.

From the chair next to Albert, André got up and went to his mother. He said, "Hey, ma chère Momma, come and join us in our discussion." He laughed. "We're talking about international politics, and we want to know what you think."

My mother stopped. To look up at him she had to lean her entire body back, and she lost her balance; André reached out for her to steady her.

She said, "Me? You want me, what is it?, that's about, what?, politics, I don't know."

"Come and join us. Tell us what you think."

She laughed a little. Her staring eyes shone. "You want me to?"

"Of course."

"Me?" She laughed again. "All right, sure I'll come, sure, I'll tell you."

Leaning on André's arm, she went towards Albert, who rose from the rocking chair, and she sat in it; only the tips of her big slippers touched the floor. Albert sat in a chair by her.

"So what do you want me, let's see, politics."

Softly, Richard said, "You tell us, Mère, what we should do to set the world right."

114

"Tell us," André said.

"Well now, I'll tell you." Her small blue eyes shifted about; she put her fingers to her smiling mouth. "Serious, now, yes, let's see."

Albert sat back; he ran his tongue over his teeth, then sucked them.

She began to laugh, and the laughter expelled the words. She said, "Total anarchy." She raised her narrow hands up, her arms wide. "Total."

André laughed. "There you are. You've said it."

Albert said, "Vous voyez comme vous êtes sage?" He pinched her ear lobe and shook her head. "Vous voyez?"

"Ah oui," she said, "je suis sage."

"It's good to see you laugh, Ma," Richard said. "It's been so long—" He stopped.

A silence descended.

My mother drew her wrinkled lips together and, her hands in her lap, went still.

André said, "Père would have liked to hear you laugh, Mère. He would have. You know how he wanted you to laugh and be happy."

"Yes, he did," she said.

"He always wanted you to be happy," Richard said.

Startling us, she placed her thumbs, fingers splayed, to her temples, and she stuck out her tongue.

"Hey, ma chère Mère," André exclaimed.

She looked at him; she appeared to be wondering what to do next.

"Ma chère, chère Momma," André said.

Again, she pressed her thumb to her nose, waggled her fingers, and stuck out her tongue.

Everyone, together, laughed.

"I'll be happy," she said. "You'll all see. I'll be happy."

I took my suitcase, which had been left by the kitchen

stove, into Edmond's room, and I sat on Edmond's bed, piled with coats and hats.

André came in. "Are you all right?" he asked.

"A little tired."

"I know what it is to travel long distances."

"Yes. You've travelled a lot in the Navy."

He smiled. "I rather like going to different places."

"Very different," I said.

"I want to show you something," he said.

On the bed was an aeroplane satchel; André unzipped it, took out a tissue-wrapped bundle, and drew back the tissue from a cylindrical silver object, embossed and studded with blue stones.

"I brought it up because I thought you'd like to see it," he said. "I thought you'd be interested."

"Thanks."

He picked it up by a black wooden handle: a decorated silver cylinder with a silver tassel dangling at the bottom edge. He handed it to me. As I swung it round, the tassel made it go faster. When it stopped, I examined it.

"It's beautiful," I said.

"Isn't it?"

"It does seem to come from far, from a strange country."

"It does."

I gave the prayer wheel back to him.

I asked, "Where have you travelled to most recently?"

Albert was sitting by his mother. She, in the rocking chair, rocked lightly by moving her body back and forth. She talked, in an undertone, lightly, as she rocked, without stopping. Albert said, "Um," as he read the evening paper.

At the table with cups of tea, I asked Julien, "How are you?"

"I'm fine," Julien said; "I'm all right."

"I know you work in a brokerage firm, but the fact is I don't quite know what you do."

"Oh, it's work," Julien said. "As I guess your writing is."

"I guess it is." I drank down the rest of my tea. I didn't know what to say. "It's very late for me," I said. "I think I should go to bed."

"You should."

"Where are we going to sleep?"

"I'm not sure."

Albert lowered his paper when I went to him and said, "You're the one who's organized everything, so I thought I should ask you where I'm supposed to sleep."

"I hadn't thought," Albert said. "Some are going to Aunt Claire's for the night, some are coming up to the country house to spend the night with me and—"

"What?" my mother asked.

"Daniel's wondering where he'll sleep," Albert said, loudly, to her.

"Don't go to bed just yet," she said to me. "Sit with us."

I sat on a kitchen chair.

"Tell me about London," she said. "Tell me how you spend, well, if you want, that's all right if you don't, can you?, want to, your day."

My voice was low with fatigue. I said, "Of course I'd like to tell you."

She said, "Now, they there, the English, do they, in England, drink more, that is, tea, do they?, than we do here?, or not?, because we do, though, a lot, who said?, and here we have it in bags, and there in pots, but then, you know, if you make it in a pot, what happens?, you have, almost always, some left in the pot, with the bags, am I explaining myself?, maybe not, let me try to explain, is this boring you? I'll try to be quick, let's see, five cups, say, five tea bags, but how many cups do you make in a pot?, you never know, so you make, that is in the pot, too much, or sometimes too little, but mostly too much, as I remember from when I used a pot once or twice, no more, and what do you do with it after? in the winter especially, when we don't drink iced tea, and you can't reheat it?, you have to throw it out, that's what, but I'll bet you use a pot anyway, in England, not bags, am I making myself clear?"

"I do use a pot, yes."

"Then how do you know, well, I guess you can get used to it, but if you miscalculate, what do you do with the left-over tea?"

Quietly, Albert said to me, "She talks non-stop now. She doesn't really listen to what you say, so you don't have to respond. Just sit by her and let her talk and from time to time say, 'Is that right, Mère?', or 'That's right'."

"What?" my mother asked.

"I was telling Daniel where he'll sleep," Albert said.

"Where?"

Albert said to me, "Why don't you and Julien stay in the middle room?"

"Where?" my mother asked, frowning.

Albert said, "Daniel and Julien will sleep in the middle room."

My mother stopped rocking. "That's where your father died," she said.

"Yes," Albert said.

She looked about me, as if there were, behind me, a larger person whom she was addressing. "Will you sleep in the bed he died in?"

I said nothing.

"Come now, Mère," Albert said. "That's not going to bother Daniel."

She said, "I slept in it the night after he died. I thought, well, I'd better, it'll help me get used to his dying, I'll lay his ghost if I do."

"It took her hours to make the bed right for her to sleep in it," Albert said. "The sheets had to be smoothed out so there were no wrinkles, and Ed and I had to bring her her blankets and pillows from her bed in her room, and we had to tuck her in, untuck her because the blankets were too tight, tuck her in again." He smiled. "And then, half an hour after we said good night to her, she called us back and said she'd been there long enough, and wanted to go back to her own bed."

"What?" she asked.

"I'm telling Dan about Père," Albert said.

"Speak more loudly so I can hear," she said.

I leaned towards my brother. "Tell me how Dad died."

Albert said flatly, "It was no great drama. Yesterday morning, while I thought he was napping, I heard him call me, and I went into the room. He said he felt nauseous. I got him sitting up on the edge of the bed, and I called Ma to help me. She had been very helpful, very solicitous towards him in the last days. She sat on one side of Père, and I sat on the other. He was in his underwear. His body was skin and tendon and bone. His head was lowered. I asked Mère to hold him up while I went for a basin for him to puke in, but just as I got into the pantry, she called, 'He's falling, he's falling,' and I ran back and grabbed him. We sat on either side of him and held him, and he sputtered a little, as if he were trying to spit, and his head fell and he went grey. I asked Mère to call the rescue squad. She was very good. She went right to the telephone, got the operator, who put her on to the rescue squad, to whom she explained clearly what had happened, and in minutes they were here. They put him on the floor and tried to revive him by thumping on his chest, but Père was gone. That was all."

"What's that?" my mother asked.

"Père had a quiet death," Albert said, leaning close to her and speaking loudly.

"Yes, he did," she said, "he did." She looked into the distance and began, again, to rock lightly.

"His dying was nothing," Albert said, "just a detail."

"He died a quiet death," Reena Francoeur said.

"And what did he die of?" I asked.

"I don't really know," Albert said.

"I won't go to the wake tomorrow," my mother said. "I don't think I'll be up to it."

"You do exactly as you wish," Albert said. "I've told you to do just that."

"I said goodbye to him lying on the bed where he died," she said. "I've already said goodbye to him."

"Again, you do as you wish, Mère."

She asked me, "What do you think? Do you think I should go to the wake?"

"I agree with Albert that you should do what you most want."

"What I most want—," she said.

Philip and Jenny came into the kitchen from the living room.

Philip said to my mother, "We thought we'd go back to Massachusetts for the night and come again early in the morning."

"Oh, don't go," she said. "Stay with me. Where are the others?"

"In the living room," Jenny said.

"Don't go yet. We'll all go in the living room and talk for a while. It seems so long since I've spoken to any of you. Come on, we'll sit together." She stood, Albert stood, and she put her hand on his arm. "For a while. I won't keep you long."

"We'd like that, Momma," Philip said.

As Albert took her into the long narrow living room, Chuckie rose from the large wing chair which had been my father's. My mother sat in it.

"Would you like a lap rug over your legs?" André asked.

"I would, yes."

About her, on the sofa, on the other big chairs, on kitchen chairs, on the floor, too, were her family. Tommy Walters was with them. In their midst was the low, heavy table made by my father with the help of Albert and me; on it were television magazines, a glass bowl, tea cups and spoons, and dark-lensed spectacles.

André put the lap rug about my mother's legs.

She said, "Daniel, you brought this to me from London. You're all so kind to me. You give me so much. Richard has given me so much perfume and cologne, my dresser is covered with bottles. And Albert all those nightgowns and housecoats, all in my drawers and closet. And Edmond, slippers and slippers. All of you, you've given me so much. Well, that's enough of that. What else shall we talk about?"

Laughing, André said, "Why don't you tell us about the sons you had and kept secret from us? Tell us about them. It's about time, isn't it?"

"Oh yes, sure, I should tell you about them, so many of them, no one knew." She smiled.

"Where are they, Ma?" Richard asked.

"All over, all over the world. But I'm not going to tell you about them. That's going to be my secret."

"Listen to her," Philip said. He was crouched by her on a hassock.

Edmond said, "Well, I know I'm the orphan of the family, aren't I?"

"That's right," my mother said; "we found you on the doorstep."

He laughed. "You see," he said to Tommy, "didn't I tell you?"

"But however many more there were, and wherever you came from, you seven are my favourites. You always have been and you always will be. Now take Julien. He's not really my last born."

"I'm not?" Julien said.

"No, oh no. Before you were born, I thought, well, I've had enough, I won't keep any more, I'll send this one out into the world right away, but when I saw you I decided, no, I want him, he'll be my last. The others that came after I sent out. Well, I kept you all because I wanted you. Your father left that up to me. I made the decision to have you all." She smiled. "Now that's enough of that conversation. What else can we talk about?"

André said, "You're not giving us much chance to talk, Momma dear."

"Well, then, speak up. If you have something to say, speak up."

I said quietly to Philip, "I'm amazed."

"It is amazing, isn't it?"

"Why don't you tell us about your travels before we were born, the way you used to when we were kids?" Philip said.

She pursed her lips, thinking.

Sitting on the carpet by Philip, Jenny said, "I've never heard one of your travel stories."

"Well, it's been a long time since I've travelled," she said, "and my memory isn't too good."

"Think back," Richard said. "I'd like my kids to hear."

"Well, I don't know, did I ever tell you about, stop me if I did, this country I went to, a long time ago, you won't believe it, you'll think I've made it up, you'll think, well, she doesn't know the world, she doesn't really know, but I do know it, I've been around the world, I've been to places none of you has heard of, and you won't have heard of this country, where I went, I'm being serious, you know how serious I can be, listen to me, I went to this country where everyone walks backwards, I swear, I swear to you, they never go forward, only backwards, so, let's see, they approach one another backwards when they meet, and to shake hands they stick their arms out behind them, and when they sit down to eat they sit facing away from the table—"

Albert said, "There's no stopping her now."

Chuckie collected the cups from the low table and went out with them and came back with a tray of many cups, each with the string and tab of the tea bag hanging over the rim. Richard took it from her, and she went out again for a steaming kettle, a carton of milk, sugar bowl and spoons. While my mother talked, Chuckie handed out cups of tea.

My mother said, "Well, that's enough of that. I'll bet you're all tired now and want to go to bed. Daniel, you must be tired."

"I am, a little," I said.

"You've come from a long way."

"But not so far as you've been."

She said, "I've been to very far places. But enough of that. Where are you all going to sleep? How we used to live in this house, the nine of us, when we were all together, I don't know. We did, though."

I stood. "I really must go to sleep."

"You go," my mother said.

Edmond stood, too. He said, "Before we separate, I want to tell you all, I want to warn you all, that tomorrow, at the wake, I'll break down."

"I won't go to the wake," my mother said. "I don't think I'll be up to it."

I kissed her on both cheeks. I said, "As we said, Momma, you must do as you want."

"I will. I will do that."

Edmond followed me out, then went before me to light the light in the middle room. He placed my suitcase on the desk.

"Is there anything I can get for you, brother?" he asked. "I've made up the beds."

"I'm sure I have everything. I'm very tired, and must sleep."

"You sleep, my brother." He put his hand around my neck and kissed me near an ear. "You sleep in your old room."

"Yes."

"It'll be like old times, sharing your old room with Julien."

"Yes."

Edmond looked around. "Well, if I can do anything—"

"Thanks."

"I'll let you be now, you must be tired."

"I am."

Edmond, leaving, shut the door slowly. "It's like old times, isn't it?"

"Yes."

"We're all together, and Mère is her old self. It would make Père happy to see us together, to see her laughing in our midst."

Naked, I looked in the closet for an old woollen bathrobe I remembered hanging on a hook at the back. As I was taking it from the hook the bedroom door opened, and my brother Richard, followed by Chuckie, came in. They turned away, and I put on the bathrobe hurriedly.

"Come in, come in," I said.

Richard said, "I'm sorry, we left our coats in here."

Chuckie took the coats from the closet. She handed her husband his, and as he put it on I noticed that he was weeping.

He said to me, "I don't know how Mère and Père did it, bring us up to be good."

Chuckie said to him, "Don't reproach yourself. You've done a good job."

Richard sighed.

He asked me, "You're spending the night here, are you?" He looked around the small room.

"And you?" I asked.

"We'll go up to Albert's," Chuckie said.

"Go to bed," Richard said to me. "You look tired."

He grabbed my shoulder and pressed it.

"I am."

The bathroom was dirty, and smelled.

Back in the room, crowded with old furniture, I stood in the middle of the floor. Against one wall, by a sewing machine, was one bed; at an angle across the room was the bed, smaller than the other, on which my father had died. I thought: I can't sleep there. Then I thought: Of course you can. I took off the bathrobe and forced myself to get under the sheet and blankets of the small bed. I lay still. I wept.

I woke when I heard my brother Julien come in, undress, and get into bed, and I fell asleep again.

With a start, I woke in silence and darkness, and I did not know where I was. I orientated myself by faint light between the slats of the window blind, and I knew that someone was standing outside the window. My pulse beat. I whispered, "Stop it, stop it."

I heard, from other rooms in the small wood-and-plaster house, the footsteps of many people. Julien's bed was empty. I knew I must get up and go out.

The robe held about myself, I went out. No one talked, but moved about one another. Albert, walking around, tied his thin black tie.

The bathroom door was shut. Passing by, Richard said to

me, "Mère's in there with Chuckie. She's decided to go to the wake after all, and Chuckie's helping her get ready."

"I can wait," I said.

The door opened and a smell of powder and cologne came out on steam from the bathroom with a slight smell of urine.

"You're coming to the wake," I said to my mother.

"I will, yes. I decided I would, for ten minutes, before the crowds come. I made up my mind to come."

Chuckie, from behind, was supporting her elbows. She winked at me over my mother's head.

"Now I've got to get dressed," my mother said. "I can't remember the last time I had a dress on, when was it?, oh yes, I know, when I went to the doctor's, well, that wasn't a very good reason for putting a dress on, now what dress will I wear?"

Supporting her as she walked, Chuckie said, "You've got so many pretty dresses. You should choose a pretty dress. We'll go to your room to choose one."

I went into the bathroom. I wanted to be alone. Someone knocked on the bathroom door and I said, "I'll be right out." When I opened, Jenny, outside, was blushing.

In my bedroom, I dressed slowly.

My brothers, and more nephews and nieces, and Tommy Walters, were in the crowded kitchen. Some had overcoats on. André, in a black overcoat, carried his white, black-visored cap under his arm. Silent, we stood about, turned away from one another.

Edmond said, "I wanted to make one request to my brothers."

"What's that, Ed?" André asked.

Edmond remained silent for a moment, and he sniffed. "Just this—"

"Come out with it," Albert said. "How are we to know what you want until you come out with it, man?"

126

"It's this—"

In a low sad voice, Richard said, "Tell us."

"I remember carrying Mémère's coffin. Dad wanted her grandsons to carry her, wanted his sons to carry his mother. I remember I broke down and cried and almost dropped the corner. Let's see, how many were there of us? Daniel and Julien, and—"

"Come on, Ed," Albert said.

"Well, I wondered if Dad's grandsons could carry his coffin, his grandsons and Tommy. That's what I'd like to know."

Philip said, "I'd like to carry my father."

"Well," Edmond said, "I just wondered."

"Listen, if it'd please you, Ed," Philip said, "of course."

"It would."

"I'll arrange it," Albert said.

"Thanks," Edmond said.

"What about his grandsons?" André asked. "And Tommy? Do they want to?"

"I've already talked about it with them all, and they said they would, yes, they'd be honoured to."

Richard put his hand on Edmond's shoulder. "We'll do as you want," he said.

I looked at Julien, who smiled, and I smiled back. We brothers smiled at one another past Edmond, who was talking to Tommy and five nephews, together with his nieces, in a group. They remained separate, a group of the young, blond, the hair of both my nephews and nieces long; they talked quietly among themselves.

"Well, here she is," André said. "Here's our mother."

Chuckie and Jenny at either elbow, our mother came into the kitchen. She was wearing a long-sleeved dark blue dress, a white cardigan, and a white woollen toque. She was talking.

"I have prettier dresses, but this, well, I think anyway, is the best, not black, I don't think I have to wear black, but not bright, either—"

André went to her and kissed her. "You look beautiful, Momma, you look so very, so very very beautiful."

She smiled.

"I was thinking," she said, "I'd have my hair done properly, I haven't been to a hairdresser in, oh, years, I think, and, well, I'll dress up, and put on make-up."

"You do that," André said, "and we'll go out."

"Will we? Well, why not? Yes. We'll go out."

Albert said, "If you want to go out, go anywhere, all you have to do is tell me, and we'll go."

"That would be nice. Now let's see, where could we go?"

"You could come and visit each of us," Philip said.

Richard said, "You could come and stay, stay as long as you like, with all your sons."

"That would be nice."

"You've never seen my apartment in Boston," Julien said.

"I could come to Boston."

"I'd take you," Julien said.

"And maybe I'll go to stay with Daniel in London. Wouldn't that be something, now, going to London?"

"I'd love you to come," I said. "I would."

She laughed. "I think you're all worried that I would come, me, an old woman."

"Now stop that, Mère," Albert said.

"I was joking," she said. "I was only joking. Don't you like me to joke?"

"Of course we want you to joke," André said.

"Well," she said, "maybe I'd like to go travelling now, go far, go to countries no one, not anyone, has heard of, what about that?, and I'd come back and tell you about it, and—"

"She's come out of herself," Albert said.

Edmond said, "Isn't it about time we got to the funeral home?"

Albert held the kitchen door open for André to help my mother down the linoleum-covered steps of the entry, and out. The others followed. I, the last, said, "You go, Albert," and Albert said, "No, you go, I've got to lock up the house." I waited by him outside on the cement stoop as he locked the back door.

Albert said, "I don't know what we're doing. This ritual of waking doesn't mean a thing."

"You arranged it all," I said.

"Yes, I did." He set his jaw.

There was a convoy of cars parked by the kerb. André signalled to me through the closed window of one, and I got into the back seat. Our mother sat between us. Julien drove.

My mother did not stop talking. Her voice was calm and light.

The New England morning was cold blue, and the houses and fences and bare trees appeared to have fine frozen edges. Julien drove to the end of June Street, the street our family house was on, to an avenue, and across from a liquor store, a coin-op laundromat, a pizza house on the avenue, was the funeral home, a brick house with shrubs before it and a parking lot on either side, and tenements beyond the parking lots. On the lawn of the funeral home was a large wooden sign incised with gold letters: VANASSE FUNERAL HOME. Julien stopped before it.

André and I helped our mother out of the back seat of the car and up the cement path. She stopped talking. She took the cement steps one at a time, we sons holding her elbows. As we approached the glass-paned door, it opened slowly.

The mortician, tucking his green tie into his grey jacket, said quietly, "Hello, Mrs Francoeur."

She said, "Hello."

He held out a hand. "You go this way," he said.

I began to tremble. I held on to my mother. We walked down a short passage and into a grey room with rows of folding chairs, and as we entered it I saw, in a coffin before bouquets of flowers, the back of my father's head on a white pillow, and I let go of my mother and walked away, to the far side of the room, trembling more, my hands over my face.

When I looked round, I saw my brothers about the coffin. André was with my mother, standing close to my father, and she put out a hand and placed it on my father's hands, folded, with a rosary, at his waist. Julien, among my brothers, turned away from the coffin, his arms out as if to reach for someone, and I went to him quickly and held him as he wept. Around us, my brothers embraced. Albert stood away, his weight on his heels, and stared beyond us.

My mother said, "He isn't cold."

André took her to an armchair at the head of a line of folding chairs along the wall of the parlour. She sat up straight in it. Her face was stark.

I went to my father. His skin was yellow and matt, and there was on his thin face a grim smile, and indentations on his cheeks where the mortician had pressed his fingers to make him smile. His hair was bright white.

An arm over my shoulders, Richard leaned on me to look at our father with me, and he said, softly, "He was a handsome man."

I heard Albert say to my mother, "Would you like to go home now?"

"I'll stay," she said.

She sat up straight as the relatives, large and dark, speaking English with French-Canadian accents, leaned down to kiss her and speak, then pass along the line of her sons.

The pastor came in, wearing his cassock. He was younger than my older brothers, Richard and Albert. After he shook our hands, he said to my mother, "Vous devez être heureuse d'avoir une telle famille."

"What?" she asked, frowning.

"You haven't forgotten your French, have you?" he asked.

"Comment?" she said.

He smiled.

Standing before the coffin, he said a decade of the rosary, and then, putting the rosary in his trouser pocket which he had to get at through a slit in the side of his cassock, he left.

After two hours, the relatives had gone, and Albert said to my mother, "I'll take you home."

"Yes," she said in a small voice.

"Do you want to kiss Père before we go?"

"Yes," she said, "I'd like to kiss him."

Albert helped her to the coffin, and she touched her husband's forehead and leaned and kissed it; her eyes closed, she turned away, and when she opened her eyes there was in them a look of pain as for the complex world. She swallowed hard. She said to Albert, "Let's go, let's go home."

At home, Jenny and Chuckie helped her to undress and once more get into her blue housecoat. She sat, in the big wing chair, in the living room.

She said, "I haven't spoken yet to my grandchildren."

"Here we are, Mémère," said Antonia.

"Tell me what you're all doing. Are you all here?"

One of Richard's sons said, "Not all, Mémère. Joseph isn't here."

"No? Where is he?"

One of Richard's daughters, a nurse, said, "He couldn't make it."

"I understand. Now, what're you all doing?"

Richard, from the doorway, watched for a while, then he went into the kitchen. His brothers and wife and sister-in-law were about the table.

Laughter came from the living room.

"What're they talking about?" Chuckie asked.

"I don't know," Richard said.

"Well," André said, "I'm happy for Momma, I really am, I'm happy that she's happy, whatever the reason."

"Yes," Philip said.

Edmond said, "I didn't break down at the wake."

"Be strong," André said to him.

"Well," Edmond said, "I'm not strong like Albert."

There was more laughter from the living room.

Richard said, "You know what I think about Ma? I think she feels, I'm free at last, free at last."

"Yes," I said.

Richard said, "They were so mismatched, our mother and father, so utterly."

He got up from the table and went into Edmond's room and half closed the door.

After a while, I went to the door, and, leaning, looked beyond it. Richard was on a chair by the bed. Light fell on him through the blind at his back. His legs were crossed, and on one knee was a small piece of paper on which he seemed to be drawing. He looked up, saw me, and said, "What is it, Dan?"

"I wondered if you're all right."

"Thanks. I am."

I continued to stand at the door.

"Come in," he said.

I sat on the bed.

"I'm sketching out an idea for a gauge," he said in a low voice.

"What kind of gauge?"

"You'd really like to know?"

"Yes, I would."

He looked at me for a moment. "And you, are you all right?"

"I am."

As he told me about the gauge, his eyes filled with tears.

He said, "You know, I remember when I was studying mechanical drawing and I'd come home and discuss my ideas with Dad. He understood. He even made suggestions. Then a day came when I realized that though he was listening, he didn't understand. He didn't say anything. I had to stop discussing ideas for my work with him because I knew he wouldn't ask me to explain."

My Aunt Oenone took the place of my mother for the evening at the wake. Large, she stood, her own hair wild under the neat false braid, before the chair my mother had sat in, and she introduced to her nephews relatives we did not know, cousins and second cousins. As an old man with a plaid woollen shirt and spectacles which magnified his eyes came towards her, Oenone held out her arms to him and said, "Polidore," and she held him closely. Oenone introduced us to Polidore Francoeur, a remote cousin. The unknown relatives passed by my father in his coffin and formed a line to give his sons their condolences.

For me, they brought with them a crude air as of a settlement in the woods of people of strange blood, a settlement which was not really a success: the cabins were falling apart, the chimneys of the wood stoves were rusting, the cooking pots had holes, and, soon, the settlement would be abandoned, but no one in it knew where to go. They had not really expected the settlement to be a success, but, now, they did not know what to do, and perhaps they would do nothing; or perhaps they would go to a city, where, somehow, they would continue to live in the woods.

I heard my aunt say in French, "He's with his mother. She taught him everything she knew. He's with her. I know he wanted to be back with her. She's teaching him what she knows now. I'll wake up one night and see them together."

I noticed Richard abruptly step out of the line as towards him came a young man. Richard met his son Joseph in the middle of the parlour, and they stood before one another, then embraced. I saw the face of my nephew, his eyes closed, over the shoulder of my brother. Chuckie stepped from the end of the line and went to them quickly, and, by them, she put her hand to her lowered forehead. The father and the son separated. Joseph embraced his mother. The three went into a room at the back of the parlour.

Next to me, Philip said, "That was Joseph."

"I saw," I said.

Joseph's brothers and sisters went to the door at the back of the parlour, but did not go in.

There were not many relatives. They took places, with my father's brother and two other sisters, the last of a family of fourteen, on the folding chairs, and they talked.

I left my brothers to go to the side of the parlour, and I looked at my relatives, and my uncle and aunts, at my brothers, and beyond them my father's body.

I thought: My father—

My father was born, as I was, among the ghosts of a small community of people of strange blood. They were people who saw that they were born in darkness and would die in darkness, and who accepted that. They spoke, in their old French, in whispers, in the churchyard, among the gravestones, in the snow, and with them, silent, were squaws with papooses on their backs, and the woods began beyond the last row of gravestones. They were strange to me, and yet they were not strange.

Their religion was my religion, the religion of a God who spoke an old parochial French, who said "moué" and "toué" for "moi" and "toi", "ben" for "bien", "à c't'heure" for "maintenant", "broyer" for "pleurer". In his old French, God talked to us about sin, ashes, the devil and hell. In English, he was strange. But not in French. When I thought about him and his religion in French, he and his religion were familiar. I prayed to my Canuck God.

Seigneur, Seigneur, ayez pitié pour nous.

It was a religion, not of recourse, but stark truth: death is what we live for, and as terrible as it is, to die is better than to live. Those of the religion were honest, and they were noble, and my heart bled for them.

There was so little the Lord could do. His heart, too, bled. He saw, he saw the whole of the past, the present, the future, and he did nothing to alter what he saw, but wept for what he saw. It was not God's fault, and it was not our fault, our condemnation; that was the way it was, because we were born condemned, most of us anyway, though we were, ourselves, innocent. We suffered as innocents. No one was to blame, not even God. It was all so vast. It was vast and it did not allow much pity, and no consolation. I would die, I would be left out, as my brothers, my sisters-in-law, my nephews and nieces, my aunts and uncle and cousins and distant cousins, as my mother, too, would be, as, no doubt, my father was, left out, and there was nothing I, as there had been nothing my father, could do.

I went out of the parlour into the cloakroom.

I was drawn to my religion. I was drawn to it because it was beyond human feeling, and human thought.

In the doorway at the back of the parlour, I saw Joseph, his mother and father, his sisters and brothers around him.

In the morning, I found my mother wandering about, talking. She did not talk to anyone in particular, but to everyone

135

she met in the crowded house. As I went to her to kiss her good morning, she said to me, "Well, so many people will be coming after the Mass, we've never had so many people, at one time, in the house, well, that's all right, except I hope no one smokes, but, well, I can go out, I guess," and she didn't stop when I kissed her, but, in her dressing gown, wandered away from me, talking. Her sister Claire came behind her and said to her, "Will you come back to your room with me? We'll never get you dressed." She said to me, "She's been talking non-stop." I smiled. Aunt Claire said, "She's not going to the Mass, but she wants to look nice when everyone comes back to the house after." She shook her head, and went after her sister.

Albert announced, "The limousines will be here soon."

At the funeral parlour, I stood with my brothers before our father, and prayed with them; then we stood to the side and waited. On the folding chairs were our uncle and three aunts, their heads lowered. When, through my tears, I glanced along the line of my brothers I saw that, at the end, Albert was a step behind us, his weight on his heels, his arms folded, staring out. I heard my brothers' breaths heave, and often they blew their noses. A tissue I held was wet and a little slimy, and I shredded it trying to open it to blow my nose. Tears dripped from my nose, my cheeks, my jaw.

I saw come into the parlour Italian neighbours, a husband and wife who lived across the street from us. They came in quietly, as if they did not quite belong there, said prayers at the coffin, and as they looked about André went to them. We others followed to shake Mr Monaldi's hand and embrace Mrs Monaldi, whose eyes filled with tears.

André said, "Siete voi, nostri parenti."

"You grew up with ours," Mr Monaldi said. "Of course we're all family, of course."

Mrs Monaldi said, "You're good boys, good boys."

They went to the back of the room to sit.

We sons reassembled in a line to the side of the coffin, and looked at our father. I was between Philip and Julien, and I heard them weeping.

Richard, next to Philip, said to him quietly, "Albert believes this is no longer Dad, but just a body. Dad's soul is elsewhere. His soul is everything, his body nothing. Perhaps Albert is right."

"Perhaps," Philip said.

I tried to hold my sudden sobs back. I bent over and pressed my fists to the sides of my head. Julien put his arms around me and held me, bent over, against his chest. Julien was weeping.

"Everything will be all right, Dan," he said. "Dad would have said, 'Everything will be all right, tsi gars. Everything will be all right.'"

He rocked me in his arms.

I said, sobbing, "The last he said to me was, 'Be a good boy.'" Then, with a little jolt, I felt that I was being dramatic, and my sobbing stopped. I drew away from Julien.

Edmond left the line to go to my father's coffin. He stood looking down at my father's face. When he sniffed, his nose and lips twitched.

He said, "And the last you said to me, Père, was, 'You've been a good boy. Thanks and goodbye.'"

He paused, as if waiting for a reaction from himself; there was no reaction, and he returned to the line.

Philip said to Richard, "You know, Dad would never compliment any one of us directly on whatever we'd achieved never, and yet he'd go on and on, proud of your achievements, to me, as I'm sure he'd go on about mine to you, but never directly."

André, on the other side of Richard, said, "Yes, that's right."

"He was a complex man," Richard said.

"He was a complex and a simple man," Philip said.

The mortician started to call out, from a list, the names of those who were to go out to their cars, beginning with the Monaldis.

Philip was called with his family. He, with Jenny and his two daughters, went to the coffin. Philip leaned over his father's head, kissed his forehead, and turned away, weeping, his folded handkerchief held up to his face. He lost balance, and his wife took his arm; she and their daughters stayed close to him as they left.

With my other brothers I approached my father's body. Julien drew back from us. As in a sudden panic, he said, "I can't touch him. I can't." He sobbed, and André held him. Richard, with Chuckie by him, kissed his father, and, shaking his head, he left weeping. Edmond kissed his father, pressing his lip for a long while to his cheek. Leaning over my father's face, I thought, I can't, I can't, but kissed his forehead, and left on it the effluence of my tears and mucus. I stepped away, and my shivering gave way to sobbing; both Julien and André came to me to put their hands on my shoulders. André said, in a clear strong voice, "Dad loved you. He did love you." I said, "Yes, yes, I know." Julien said, "He loved us all." André went to kiss his father. Albert, at the exit, waited for his brothers to go out, and he left last; he stayed away from his father's body.

We got into the limousine, parked by the kerb. Before us was the hearse. We watched, in silence, the grandsons and Tommy carry the coffin down the cement steps of the funeral home, to the sidewalk, and place it on a metal frame which swung out from the side of the hearse and was swung back in. The mortician closed the hearse door.

Albert, by me on the jump seat, said, "Sa mission est accomplie."

The coffin appeared through the back window of the hearse. The hearse started.

Edmond said, in a burst of tears, "There he goes."

Albert said, "Tais-toi."

"God gave us tears to relieve us of what we can't bear," Richard said. Chuckie was sitting by him. "At least he gave us that."

"Yes," Albert said, "you're right."

Sniffling, Edmond said, "I thought I was going to break down. I didn't. I don't know why I didn't."

The church was very cold, the air in it still and smelling slightly of damp. In the first two rows, the sons, wives, daughters, knelt, then stood as the coffin, on a metal frame, was wheeled to the altar rail, followed by the pallbearers. The mortician showed the pallbearers into a pew. From the sacristy came the curé and an assistant priest, both in long white chasubles with narrow black crosses on the front and back. The assistant held a brass pot of holy water and the curé sprayed the coffin with the holy water sprinkler; the water dripped off the edges of the coffin.

The curé said, "We commend the soul of Arsace Louis Pylade to you, Lord—"

I thought: He has gone into the woods.

As we followed the coffin out of the church, the bell tolled. The winter morning of the American North was bright.

In the limousine, Edmond laughed. He said, "I was thinking, Ma always says that when she's buried we'd better bury her upside down, because she won't be dead, she'll refuse to die, and she'll try to dig her way out, but she'll be digging herself deeper in. So if we don't want her back, we'd better bury her upside down."

Albert said, severely, "She won't have much to say about that."

We entered the Catholic cemetery.

The coffin was brought by the bearers into a stark chapel with plain yellow windows, and placed on a white cloth-covered stand, behind which the assistant priest, a young man, said prayers. There was no burial; the coffin was left in the chapel. Leaving, I touched it.

I found André by the chapel door. He was weeping. He said, "I don't know, Dan, it's all right and it's all wrong." I put my arm around him and we went out of the chapel.

No one spoke in the limousine.

Then Albert said, "There're a number of things I want to do on Mom's house. One of the windows is cracked, a faucet in the pantry leaks, and one of the light switches doesn't work."

The silence was deep among his brothers.

"Remind me, will you, Julien, to buy a new light switch."

"I will," Julien said.

"And the house needs to be painted, inside and out," Albert said.

In the kitchen, platters of caterer's sandwiches and pastries were spread over the table, and on a counter by the stove was a big enamel urn of coffee with paper cups, flat wooden spoons, a bowl of sugar cubes and a plastic pitcher of milk.

Albert remained in the kitchen to put out napkins and paper plates.

Our overcoats on, the other sons went into the living room to our mother, who, dressed, was in the wing chair. Her sister Claire was by her. In turn, we bent and kissed her, and rose in tears. She appeared a little bewildered.

André hugged her closely. "Oh, Momma," he said.

I took their coats and went into the middle room to put

them on a bed. I found Richard there, his shoulders a little hunched, looking at the photographs on the walls.

"I'm glad about Joseph," I said to him.

"We'll see," Richard said. "We'll see."

He put his arms about me and held me.

II

IN THE CROWDED living room, some sat, some stood about Reena Francoeur.

"Where's Edmond?" she asked.

"He's in the cellar with Tommy and some of his nephews and nieces, running his trains," André said.

"Sometimes I think he's a little too old, fifty what?, how old is Edmond?, playing with trains, but he could do worse."

"He's all right, Ed is," Philip said.

"His trains are the world to him," she said. "He doesn't go anywhere, stays home. It's only with his trains that he goes anywhere."

Richard said, "I think we should get going. We've got a long drive ahead of us."

"Right," Chuckie said.

Richard looked over to the far end of the living room, where, standing by a floor lamp, were Albert and Joseph, talking.

He asked Chuckie, "Do you think Joe'll want to come with us?"

"I don't know."

Reena said, "Where is Joe?"

Chuckie called, "Joe, your Mémère wants to speak to you."

Joseph came over. His body was big, and he walked with a

slight jaunt. His hair was receding. "What's up?" he asked.

"Now, Joe," his Mémère said, "I wanted to tell you, but I don't want your mother and father to hear, so lean over, I'll whisper, I want to tell you something."

Joseph leaned, his ear near her mouth.

She smiled and whispered.

Joseph shook his head. "Mémère!"

"There it is."

He laughed and kissed her.

"Are you coming back with us?" Chuckie asked him.

"No, I don't think so."

"All right."

"Uncle Albert said I could stay with him," Joseph said.

"Don't go," his grandmother said to him. "Stay with us for a while longer so we can talk."

"We'll stay," Richard said.

Albert asked, "Who'd like a cup of tea?"

"I'll get it," Julien said.

"We'll do it together."

My mother said, "There were many, yes, well not many, but some jokes I used to play on all you boys, let's see, is this an interesting conversation or not?, am I boring you?, jokes, well, your father didn't like them very much, that is he liked them, but not very much, he never stopped us though, at the supper table he didn't like us to joke, but he didn't stop us there, we did, not too much, but we did, a little—"

"I used to think," Richard said, "that if Momma died first, Dad wouldn't survive her for long."

"What?" their mother asked, loud.

"We were talking about Père," Richard answered.

"What about him?"

"We were just talking about him."

"He didn't like the joke we played at the supper table, this joke, do you remember?, I'd say, now look at my nose without laughing, try to do it without laughing, and no one could, no one could look at my nose without laughing, finally, I'd say, 'Well, it's just a nose, what's so funny?', but your father didn't like us to joke at the supper table—"

Albert and Julien came in with the tea and placed it on the low table. They lit the floor lamps in the winter afternoon.

Their mother continued to talk.

"He was dependent on her to the last," Philip said.

"He was, yes," Albert said.

"He was a man of strong drives."

Albert said, "It wasn't two weeks ago that he was trying to get into her bed, and she said, no, no, she didn't want to. That's the real reason why we had to put him in the middle room. He told me once, 'My marriage with your mother ended when we got single beds.' He was a man of strong drives, all right, and Mère didn't want to submit to them any longer."

She stopped talking. "What?"

"We were saying what a good husband Dad was," Richard said, laughing.

"Cut it out, Richard," Chuckie said.

He laughed more. "Wasn't he?"

His wife punched his arm.

"Oh yes," Reena said, "he was a good husband, a good husband and a good father, he worked hard, but that was his nature, he didn't like us to joke, I could never get him to laugh looking at my nose."

Richard said, "I don't think I ever heard him joke."

"He had his jokes," Julien said.

Philip said to Jenny, "I think we should start out before it gets dark."

"Yes," Richard said. "We'll go, too."

"You're going?" their mother said.

"We should, Mom."

144

"Where's Philip?"

"Right here." He stood.

She put her hand over her eyes to shade them from the lamp as she looked up at him.

"What can I do for you?" Philip asked.

"Well," she said, "I've been wanting to tell you, for a long time I've been wanting to tell you, I felt I couldn't when your father was alive, he couldn't understand a joke, so now, are you prepared?, I want to tell you, I want to tell you that I think that table's ugly and I wish you'd take it out of here." She laughed; she held her hands to her mouth to keep her loose false teeth in as she laughed.

Philip laughed. "I know, Momma," he said, "I know."

"Will you take it?"

"Yes."

"Now? Right now?"

"I'll put it in the trunk of the car and tie it down."

In the evening, André, Julien and I sat about our mother. She was tucked into her chair with the lap rug. She talked.

"Where's Edmond?" she suddenly asked in the midst of her talk.

"Gone up to the mall with Tommy," Julien said.

"And Albert?"

"He went up to his house in the country with Joseph for the night."

"And where's—"

"What is it?" André asked.

She said, "I was about to ask where your father is."

She stopped talking.

"Come on, Momma," I said, "tell us some of your jokes."

As she talked, I saw in my mother, in her small warped body with thin legs too short for her feet to touch the floor, a little girl who, out of the world now, was innocent of the world. I saw my brothers and myself as strangers in the outside world whom she found herself among, not quite sure how, and, in her innocence, she trusted us, she believed that we and the outside world must be good. And we, because we saw she was innocent, protected her.

As she talked, I reached out and put my arms around her to hug her.

Julien silently left us, and later I found him sitting up in his bed, the light on.

I undressed and got into my bed.

He asked, "How are you?"

"I don't know," I said.

"I understand."

"And you?"

He said, "I don't know either." He paused. "I had never before Dad seen anyone dead."

"No one, in almost forty years?"

"I couldn't. I never could."

"Until Dad."

"Not until Dad," he said.

The first night alone in the middle room, I slept not in the small bed, but the larger bed Julien had left. I was frightened in the calm, spacious dark. Out loud, I said, as to a presence in the dark, "Go away, go away," and forced myself to sleep. But I woke from time to time, frightened, then tears came to my eyes.

I lay still in the morning and thought of my father, his sons' kisses and tears on his face.

In the kitchen, I found my brother André saying goodbye to my mother.

André said, "Ed's going to drive me to the airport."

"Shouldn't he be working?" she asked.

"He's taken a few days off. He deserves to rest."

"Yes, he does."

"I didn't know you were leaving today," I said.

"I've got to, Dan. I've got to get back to my wife and kids."

"We haven't had much chance to talk."

"We'll talk when you come to visit. You will, won't you?"

"Yes. I will."

Edmond came out of his room. The fur earflaps of his hat were down, but the chinstrap was unbuckled. "We'd better be going," he said. He was holding his car keys.

I asked André, "Have you been painting?"

"I keep it up. You'll see when you come, the walls of the rumpus room are covered with my paintings." He laughed. "I don't know where I got it, the need to paint."

"I could ask, too, where I got the need to write," I said.

"Who knows."

"Come on," Edmond said.

"You will come and visit?" André asked me.

"I will. Yes, I will."

They left, and I sat with my mother at the table.

She said, "I really should have a bath, of course I don't expect my sons to be able to help me bathe, but I don't have any daughters, what can I do?, I don't want to depend on my daughters-in-law or my sister Claire, they're busy."

"I'll help you bathe," I said.

"What? You?"

"I'll do it if you'd like."

"I don't know." She bit her lower lip and looked at me, then smiled. "Well, all right."

I had to get from a cupboard in the front entry two towels and a face cloth, and place them on the radiator to warm. I had to place a kitchen chair in the bathroom, near the washbasin. I helped her, in the small bathroom, to take off her housecoat, and she, leaning against the washbasin and turned away from me, raised her flannel nightgown to pull

147

down her pants; they fell about her feet, in men's woollen socks and big slippers, and I asked her to lift one foot, then the other, to take them off. She sat on the chair, but had to stand again to test with the tips of her fingers if the water in the basin was too hot or too cold; she sat again. She unbuttoned the front of her nightgown and I pulled it back so her small, white, humped back showed, the vertebrae pronounced, and she held close to her the bodice of the nightgown.

She said, "Soap the face cloth, will you, and wash under my night gown. Wring out the cloth first so it isn't too wet."

Under the loose nightgown, I washed her back, reaching down to her buttocks. I rinsed the cloth and wiped her. I washed her thin neck, under her chin, and inside the bodice; she held both hands to one side to hide her mastectomy scar, and I saw her one breast, small and wrinkled.

"You go out," she said, "and I'll do the rest."

"I'll stand just outside the bathroom door," I said, "so you can call me when you want me."

Outside, I heard her talking quietly to herself.

She called me.

"Will you help me dress now?" she asked.

"Of course."

I walked before her, backwards, to hold her hands as she shuffled to her room. "I thought I'd get dressed. I thought I'd get dressed every day."

"You'll feel much better doing that, rather than staying in your nightgown and housecoat all day."

"That's what they say. I'll do what they say. It makes them happy to see me dressed, so I'll dress to make them happy."

"Who are they?"

"You all," she said. "You're all so kind to me. I think I should do something to show you that I appreciate your kindness."

"We appreciate that."

"You are kind."

"If we are, it's because we want to be, and we want to be especially when we see you respond."

"Oh yes, I know."

"It's a pleasure to be kind to you when you're in a good state."

"And it's not a pleasure when I'm in a bad state?"

"No, it isn't."

"I know."

She sat on the edge of her bed.

She said, "I'm in a good state now, aren't I?"

I combed her short hair from her face with my fingers. "You are," I said.

"Now," she said, "could you get from the drawer of my bureau my girdle? The old one, not the new one. The old one is softer."

I opened the drawer to piles of pastel-coloured nightgowns and underpants, and in a corner found an old girdle; the garter on one side was a strip of elastic with a safety pin. She stood, and I, on my knees, held the girdle open; she held my shoulder for support as she stepped into it, and I pulled it up, under her nightgown, to her hips. She stumbled back and sat, with a little bounce, on the bed.

"It has to be zipped," she said.

"I'll turn away."

I turned.

"I can't do it," she said.

I turned round to her. Her gown was raised about her waist, and she was trying to zip up the side of the girdle. Her shinbones showed through her thin yellow legs; her wrinkled flesh bulged over the stiff edges of the girdle, at her thigh and stomach. Her gown was raised so I saw the bottom of her breast.

149

"Let me," I said.

As I bent over to close the zipper, I saw, between her legs, my mother's small, finely haired pudenda. I closed the zipper.

"Now will you get some panties? Not new ones, old ones."

The slightly frayed panties I found, pale pink with little roses embroidered at the edges, were not the ones she wanted; she wanted the ones with the elastic gone at the legs. She held my head to step into them.

Next, I gave her her bra, with one cup padded. She stuffed it down into her bodice, and I, lifting her flannel gown at the back, hooked it. The strap indented her loose, crêpy flesh. There were many moles on her back.

"Stockings now," she said.

"Which?"

"The ones with the hole in the toe."

They were orange-pink. I attached the top of one to the girdle with the little pink knob and metal clip of the garter. The other stocking I pinned to the garter with the safety pin.

I helped her take off her nightgown from over her head and to put on a pink slip.

She crossed her arms and put her hands on her shoulders.

I opened the closet door to many dresses on metal hangers.

"Put on a nice dress," I said. "You've got so many."

"I know. I do."

"Which one would you like?"

"Take out the one at the back," she said.

I held up, by the hanger, a blue and silver dress; it had a metallic sheen.

"I wore that on our fiftieth wedding anniversary," she said.

"I remember."

"That's the dress I'm going to be laid out in."

Severely, I said, "Come now, Momma. I don't like hearing that."

"I'm not being morbid. I'm not. I'm just telling you." She laughed. "Put it away."

She chose a plain grey woollen dress and a woollen cardigan. She didn't want shoes, or any of the slippers from the closet; she wanted the large men's slippers she had been wearing.

As I was combing her hair Albert appeared at the bedroom door. "Here you are," he said.

"Who is that?" my mother asked.

"Albert," I said.

Albert came in, kissed my mother and asked, "Is there anything I can do for you?"

"I'm fine," she said.

I said to him, "You needn't have come down to the city today. You could have stayed in the country and rested. I can do for Momma while I'm here."

"I wanted to check out if everything was all right."

I smiled. "I hope so," I said.

Albert went out.

My mother said, "Albert does so much for me. So much. But he won't help me dress. He won't touch me. He doesn't like touching me."

"What would you like me to do for you?" I asked.

She said, "Now that I'm all dressed, I think I've got to have a bowel movement."

I helped her back into the bathroom.

Albert, at the pantry sink, was washing the breakfast dishes.

I asked, "Did Dad have an autopsy?"

Albert emptied the dishpan of water into the sink. "No. He was buried with his body intact."

151

I took a bus downtown, and walked about Providence. The cold sea wind through the narrow streets blowing about me made me aware of the outlines of my body under my overcoat, scarf, gloves.

I walked up College Hill to the low brick museum. My gloves off, my overcoat unbuttoned, my scarf loose, I wandered through the rooms I used to wander through as an adolescent, and I saw, on entering a room, beyond a doorway in the next room, suddenly around a corner, paintings and statues I had forgotten, and remembered; but, seeing them again, I couldn't locate them in my memory of the museum, but remembered them, it seemed to me, from some unlocatable place, at some unknown time.

Back in the foyer, I walked past the antique furniture to a window at the end where, on a plinth, was a torso in marble. I stood before it for a long time. Against the light from the window, it was grey-blue. The right shoulder and neck were broken off; over the left shoulder was a fragment of a cloak; the left arm was gone; where the penis had been was a soft-edged hole; the legs were broken off. I walked about it, and the light from the window on it made it white-yellow. The buttocks were chipped. I walked to the front again. The marble body was a little in torsion, as if it were turning.

I remembered.

I thought: Oh wonder—

In the late afternoon, I went to my Aunt Claire and Uncle Jake's apartment in the city, and I stayed with them for early supper.

Uncle Jake said, "Please, let's not talk about Reena. We've talked about her for years and years, and nothing we've said has come near to explaining why she is as she is, much less given us an idea of what to do to help her."

"I know," Aunt Claire said, "I know." She said to me,

"You know, she could help herself if she wanted to. I know she could. But she doesn't want to."

"Why?"

"Because she—"

Uncle Jake said, "Please."

I took a taxi across the city to June Street.

Edmond was at the kitchen table drinking a cup of tea. The house was silent. He whispered, "She's in a bad way."

"Where is she?"

He nodded towards the living room.

I took off my outer clothes and threw them over the back of a chair.

"I phoned Richard," Edmond said. "I said that I didn't know what to do, that Albert didn't know what to do. I said that we should get together, all the sons, and talk about what we can do." Edmond's voice was calm.

The living room was lit only by a dim floor lamp. I saw my mother in the near-dark, in her chair, a hand over her face. I approached her quietly and sat near her, leaning forward. She lowered her hand and stared at me, her eyes wild. Her teeth were out, and her lips pinched together. She was in her old blue housecoat.

She said, "Daniel."

"Yes," I said softly.

"Will you tell me something? Will you?"

"What do you want me to tell you, Momma?"

She stared. "What's wrong with me?"

I touched my mother's cheek. "Oh Momma."

"What?" she asked. "What? What is wrong with me?"

"I don't know."

"You don't know? Why don't you tell me? Who knows? No one tells me. I've never been a good mother, never a good wife. Tell me, tell me."

Edmond came into the room and, his arms crossed, stood over her.

"What's wrong with me? What's wrong with me? What? What?"

Edmond said flatly, "Don't pity yourself. You have no reason to pity yourself."

She slammed her small fist against the arm of the chair. "Don't tell me that. Don't. I don't want pity. I don't. I never wanted pity. I wanted to go away. I want to go away. I want to get out of here."

I shouted, "Momma, you have no reason to do this, to think only of yourself. A lot is being done for you. A lot. You've got to stop thinking of yourself."

Her hands unclenched and she let them fall on to the lap rug.

Edmond shouted, "You try doing for yourself without us. Try it. Try it. I've fixed up your bed, you can get into it yourself." Angry, he went out.

I stayed with my mother.

She said, "I remember when you used to sit with me and listen to me talk and talk. That was so many years ago, before you went away. You were so patient. You can't say you did it all for nothing, you can't. And maybe you went away to get away from me."

I saw in my mother an innocent suffering which seemed to have nothing, nothing to do with the outside world.

She said, "I wanted you to go away thinking I was better. I wanted you to go back to London thinking I'm in a good, healthy state. I'm sorry. I'm sorry. Now you'll want to go from me."

"Do you want me to go?" I asked.

An expression of shock came to her face. "What?"

"Never mind," I said. "I don't want to hear you talk this

way. It makes me feel very badly. I don't like it." I stood. "I'm going to help you to bed."

"All right," she said, "all right," as if I had told her she was being sent off alone into the world to take care of herself as best she could, and she accepted that. "All right."

I stood before her to help her up from her chair, but she made a gesture as of pushing me away, and I stepped back. I watched her, hunched, press on the seat at her sides to lift herself from the chair; standing, she staggered, then held out her arms to get her balance. Lifting her feet as if they were heavy and she had to half drag them, she stepped forward. I walked backwards ahead of her. She shuffled after me.

I thought: Please God, have pity on us—

She looked to the side, not at me. "I know," she said. "I know. It's all my fault. Everything is my fault."

From the bathroom, I walked before her into her bedroom. I drew the bedclothes down and she took off her housecoat and got in; then I sat at the edge of the bed.

"I don't know what to do," she said. "I don't know. I don't know."

"Shall we say some prayers?" I asked.

She exclaimed, "Oh will you? Will you do that for me? Will you?"

In a drawer in the bedside table I found a rosary which I knew had been her mother's.

I said, "Notre Père, qui êtes aux cieux, que votre nom soit sanctifié—"

She responded, also in French.

At the end of the first decade, she said, "That's enough."

"Will you sleep?"

"I want you to go to sleep."

In my room, I thought: My father, all throughout his life, could not think of himself, but had to think of his duty to the outside world.

155

Reena Francoeur sat in her chair, silent, her dark spectacles on against the dim light.

I sat near her.

In her bedroom, Edmond was going through her husband's belongings. Tommy Walters was with him. They were talking quietly.

Edmond called me into the room, where the doors of our father's wardrobe were open, and the drawers on one side pulled open.

"I thought you might like to take something of Père's as a remembrance of him," Edmond said.

He took out a drawer and put it on the bed. We found in it a magnifying glass; a little ivory elephant emblem of the Republican Party; a money belt with foreign coins; gold cufflinks; two gold rings; bits of mineral ore from a mine in which, before his marriage, he had invested all his savings, and lost; a tie clip; small metal capsules with smaller statues of saints in them; a pocket watch and fob; an unused billfold spread out in its thin, narrow box; a cigarette case with the names of all his sons inscribed in gold on the back; a spirit level; an old French prayerbook; a silver dollar.

I opened a cloth pouch and from it let fall into my palm blue and white enamel lapel pins. I examined them.

"I'll take these," I said.

I put the lapel pins into the cloth pouch, and the pouch into my pocket.

There was something I must do, but I did not know what it was. When I said to myself, You want to go out, I thought, No, I don't. I did not want to go anywhere, and yet I could not think what it was I had to do; what I had to do, I sensed, was in some other place, at some other time.

I wandered about the living room.

My mother said, "Daniel."

"Yes?" I asked.

"I will make an effort," she said, "you'll see, not for myself, but for your father. I will be all right."

Crouched before her, I held her hand for a while; I kissed it, and placed it on the other resting in her lap.

I said quietly, "I think I'll go out."

"Where?" she asked as quietly.

"I'll go up to the country."

"Is that where you want to go?"

I didn't answer.

"It's cold," she said; "dress warmly."

Edmond let me use his car, and as I drove I had the continuing sense of there being something I must do which I couldn't locate in place or time.

The sky was low and dark, and when I got into the country the clouds appeared to sag under their weight over the late winter woods.

The lake was covered with white, porous ice; there were cracks in it and wide channels down which ice floes floated on black water.

I got out of the car into mild, still air, and in it, on small sudden currents, were fine smells of resin, of water, of fish. Walking, they mingled about me, and I breathed them in. They were fresh and slight, and I was not sure if they were smells of resin or water or fish, for as I was about to identify them, they went. I walked around a swarm of midges towards the house.

It was closed. Of fieldstone and timber, it stood high on a knoll; the dormer windows reflected the dark clouds. I went round it. At the bottom of the knoll, near the garage, I looked up at the clouds passing, it appeared, through the windows.

Among the mild currents of air were sudden cold rushes, and I drew my arms to my sides.

I descended to the point of land which jutted out into the lake; the bridge from it to the island was reduced to cement piles and big, half-rotted beams. I hesitated, then quickly crossed on a beam, and jumped on to the shore of the island.

It was running with water; there were rivulets of water gushing through the mulch of moss, dead leaves, pine needles, and fine roots covering the ground, and it oozed about my feet as I stepped. I walked up the narrow path, through close, dark laurels and bare berry bushes, up under the bare oaks, which dripped water. The shifting winds off the lake brought me more smells, and as I felt the currents released in the air, I felt them released in the ground, felt slight but abrupt shifts about me, and I could not tell what, in the next moment, might happen.

I walked through the woods on the island; the large motionless trees stilled all movement, but it was a stillness of movement which would continue, in a sudden burst, the moment I left the woods; it was the stillness of people in the stark bare woods who, behind the tree trunks and drooping fir branches, had withdrawn as I approached, and, watching me, were waiting for me to go. I had never seen any. I stood, myself motionless, among them.

I walked on slowly, pushing aside wet branches. At my thighs and calves, my trousers were wet; water seeped into my shoes. At times the path disappeared, and I pressed myself through bare bushes covered with red berries, then found the path, and continued along the long, narrow, wooded island,

158

around outcroppings of granite, fallen trees, tangles of thorny vines. In the stillness of the woods there was the calm, clear space of a strange country, and though I could not see it or hear it, and did not know what went on in it, I knew it was populated. The light began to vivify as I walked, making the calm space among the trees clearer. The island narrowed to a path with water and ice on both sides, then widened again to rock; in the cracks of the rocks were old ducks' nests with broken eggs. The rock was surrounded by pines between which the lake showed, the ice grey-white and broken. About the bottoms of the trees were patches of snow.

As I walked back, the light darkened and the air became chill.

In almost dark, snow fell. The snow fell loosely; then, as I walked through the densest part of the woods, it revolved among the trees with a *whish* sound, and disappeared. I stood under a pine tree.

I was with my father.

David Plante is the author of six previous
novels, including *The Family* which was
nominated for a National Book Award.
His work has appeared in *The New
Yorker,* the *Paris Review* and elsewhere.
He is an American and lives in London.